REASONS
I FELL FOR
THE FUNNY
FAT
FRIEND

CASSIE MAE

REASONS I FELL FOR THE FUNNY FAT FRIEND

COOKIE Lynn

Dedicated to everyone who knows the importance of laughter and counts it as their workout for the day.

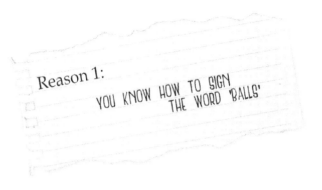

Reason 1:
YOU KNOW HOW TO SIGN THE WORD 'BALLS'

More than half the time, girls who think they're fat really aren't. They're just fatter than the skinniest chick in school. And even that girl thinks she's fat. So when Hayley, my signing partner in American Sign Language shrugs off Josh moo-ing at her as she walks in the room, that's when I figure this girl... isn't like most girls.

Fact is, Hayley isn't *really* fat. She's... I dunno. Not fat. The girls who talk about being fat look that way 'cause they wear clothes that don't fit. Like that's going to impress us guys somehow. But the muffin top is not hot.

Hayley doesn't have a muffin top 'cause she wears pants that are her size. So the moo-ing and other douchbaggery don't make sense.

Maybe it's 'cause I'm not that kind of guy. But whatever.

She plops in the seat next to me, popping her gum and twisting the brown curls hanging from her ponytail. We don't talk much. Just sign, and if she was showing the slightest bit of 'woe is me' from Josh's comment, I'd probably say something. But she's not so I don't feel like an ass for keeping my mouth shut. That, and I'm waiting for someone else to walk through that door.

Quynn.

It sucks wanting someone you can't have. And Quynn is definitely a 'don't go there'. She's my brother's ex. There's some kind of code for that shit, but that's not what's stopping me. Gabe's a cheating douche, so not sure if I'd feel too guilty about going after his ex-girl. It's Quynn. Every time we get together it's just... weird. Like she thinks I'm her brother. So yeah, sort of takes her off any list I have of girls I'll probably get to see naked. Not like there's a long list or anything.

The room is too hot. All the sweat makes my clothes stick to my balls. Man, if Quynn walks in right when I adjust myself, I may as well sniff my hand afterward too, since that's how attractive I'll look.

Okay, Brody, be quick about it. Be cool. How do you look cool when you scratch yourself? *She's still not here. Do it now! It's driving you crazy!*

One quick glance around the room and a shift later, nuts are in the right place and no one seems to have noticed. What a big deal over nothing.

"All right," Ms. Stevens says as she turns around. "It's silent time, now. Only communicate through sign. I'll be walking around to check on each of you."

She starts weaving through the desks, and finally, Quynn walks through the door. She opens her mouth to apologize, but Ms. Stevens puts a finger to her lips and motions for Quynn to take a seat. She throws me a grin and a wave as she crosses the room. Her body looks kick-ass even in a hoodie and jeans. I've only seen her in something else a few times, and that was when she was in a Prom dress—worst day of my life since I caught her and douchebag brother going at it in the parking lot. And when she came to school once, *once*, in a skirt that showed off a pair of the sexiest legs I've ever seen. I know I wasn't the only one who wasn't able to concentrate that day.

A light tap on my shoulder jerks my attention to Hayley. That's right; we're supposed to be doing an assignment or something. She smiles and starts signing.

You okay? You seem... I don't catch the rest. She's real good.

Sorry, go slower.

She smiles wider and emphasizes each movement.

2

You seem in a D-A-Z-E.

Or just slobbering over the goddess that just walked in. Same dif.

I'm fine. As fine as I ever am.

Well, what did you… bunch of gibberish.

Man, I wish I was as good as she was.

S-L-O-W!

She giggles which gets a *shhh!* from Ms. Stevens.

Sorry. Hayley blushes and turns back to me and signs so slow, her hand bounces up and down. *What do you want to talk about for the hour? I really don't want another lecture over my lack of taste in music.* She rolls her eyes so I catch the sarcasm.

No educating you then. I run my hand over my buzzed head before continuing. *How about movies this time?*

She scrunches her nose. *I don't see many movies.*

I swear this girl lives under a rock. *Why not?*

Her face goes red again, and I wonder if I overstepped a line or something. She blushes over movies but not the moo-ing? Yeah, I don't get girls at all.

Sorry, did I butt in?

She flushes deeper. Dude, what's wrong with her? Movies I guess are out. She looks around and waves me in closer, so her signs can only be seen under our desks.

It's no big deal or anything, but… more gibberish.

I grunt and stop her hands with mine. They feel kinda warm and she jerks away, going so red I don't think there's any blood in any part of her body but her face right now.

Slow, please. Maybe adding the magic word will stop her from acting so weird.

Sorry. I was saying, I don't see a lot of movies 'cause I don't go out much.

Why is that such a big deal? I wait for her to go on, but she sits straight up and starts signing so fast I'm pretty sure she's not saying anything at all.

I start for her hands again, then I get it. Ms. Stevens has a very distinct smell. I'm almost choking on the flowers wrapped in bacon stench coming from behind me. I glance at our teacher whose lips are pursed as she signs, *Are you going to answer her, Brody?*

Whoops. Hayley was way too fast for me to keep up. I lock gazes with my signing partner, and she re-signs the question.

So, who would it be? Jessica Alba or Scarlett Johansson?

Okay, if she's asking about Invisible Woman vs. Black Widow, then I know the answer, but if she's asking who's hotter, how am I supposed to answer that with Quynn looking at me from across the room?

Scarlett, I guess. My hands won't stop shaking, so that's all I say. Ms. Stevens waves in front of my face.

Work on your 'S's. She leaves, but not without me going as red as Hayley was just a few seconds ago.

Hayley clears her throat. Oh right. We were in the middle of something.

Sorry. We were talking about not going to movies. Then you pull two actresses out of your butt.

We both stifle our laughter. I sorta like it when girls think I'm funny. Does weird things to my stomach, but in a good way.

So like I was saying, I don't get to go out much. You know, because I'm just not one of those girls.

No, I don't know. I don't have the secret handbook that lets me know everything. *Girls that like to see movies?* I chuckle and she chuckles.

No. Like I'm not... She stops and does a mock thinking face. It's kinda cute. *I don't get asked out a lot.* She signs it fast, but I catch it.

How do I respond to that? It's not like we're best buds, and that's a pretty big thing to admit for a girl. Man, even for a guy, it's hard to admit. Why is she telling me?

You have friends though, right? I attempt a smile.

She nods. *They've all got boyfriends. Sitting in a theater with a bunch of people making out around me? No thanks.*

She attempts a smile. I wonder if I look as half-hearted as she does.

Yeah. I get that. Boy do I get that. I was Mr. Third Wheel around my brother.

It slaps balls.

I bark out laughing. Did she really sign that, or did I interpret it wrong? But she's laughing too, and everyone's looking at us.

"Do I need to separate you two?" Ms. Stevens asks, lips in such a tight line I wonder if it actually came from her mouth.

"Sorry. I'll try not to tell jokes anymore since Brody can't find a volume control on his laugh."

I laugh again, proving her point, but not much I can do about it since it's already out there. Quynn giggles across the room, and even though I'm getting a big fat 'see me after class' look from the teacher, it was worth it.

***

"I'll see you tomorrow," Hayley says after the bell rings. She scoops up her book and throws her bag over her shoulder, smacking me in the face.

"Whoops! Sorry."

I shove her bag out of my way and give her the not-so-serious-mad look. She laughs and waves, knocking other people over as she makes her way to the door with her over-crowded backpack.

Maybe she doesn't live under a rock, but a pile of homework.

"Brody?"

I force myself to look at Quynn slowly. If I whip around too fast, I'll look like I've been waiting for her to say my name like that. Which I have, but still. *Be cool.*

"Yeah?"

"Do you have a sec? I need to ask you something."

Why does she make me nervous? We used to hang out all the time before...well before Gabe banged another girl.

"Yeah."

Instead of letting me stand, she perches her sexy form on the top of my desk, which leaves me eye level with her chest.

Oh dude.

She smells like spicy apple. I know exactly what lotion she wears, because I'm that pathetic. She watches everyone leave the room with a big smile on her face. Damn that smile. Her eyes flick to me and everything shifts below the belt. Am I ogling? Or drooling?

I hear the door click, leaving us alone. Guess Ms. Stevens wants out of here. "Kay, so I've got a huge favor to ask you."

Look up, look up. Her eyes are just a few more inches up.

"Okay."

She reaches into her pocket. Her snug pocket. *Look up.*

"Could you give this back to Mom? I mean… your mom?"

It takes me a minute to process. And to look away from the sudden hurt in her face. Quynn was tighter with their boyfriend's mom more than I've ever seen someone else be. When I finally get a grip, I notice the bracelet Mom gave her dangling between her fingers.

"Why?" I drag the word out and fold my arms.

"Don't make me smack you, Bro. You know why."

I hate that nickname because of the stupid double-meaning. Is she calling me Bro 'cause she still thinks of me as her brother? Well, that's not a far reach, since she just called my mother, Mom.

"She won't take it back. And I'm not going to let you give it back either."

Her puff of breath nearly knocks me over with how good she smells. "Please, Bro. I know it was expensive, and I just don't feel right about keeping it."

I shake my head. She's got to be kidding me. I'm not going to get sucked into the drama more than I already have.

Another puff hits my face. "Fine." She slides off my desk and drops the jewelry into her pocket. Without another word, she's out the door.

Damn   brother   ruins   everything.

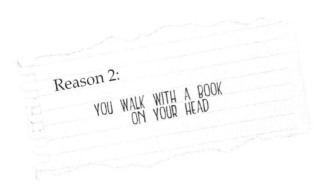

Reason 2:
YOU WALK WITH A BOOK
ON YOUR HEAD

"Hey hun," Mom says as I walk through the door. "How was your day?"

Standard Mom question.

"Fine."

Standard kid answer.

She waves me into the kitchen with a knife in her hand. Then she goes back to chopping tomatoes. I wrinkle my nose.

"You're going to eat these and be happy about it," she threatens as I sit on the bar stool across from her, letting my backpack drop to the floor by my feet.

"Yes, Mother."

She makes a face. "I hate it when you say that."

I laugh. "I know."

She picks up a tomato slice and shoves it under my nose. "Now you have to eat it. That's your punishment for being a smartass."

"Uugh." My gag reflex pumps in my throat as I push her hand back. "How about I just say I'm sorry?"

"And...?" She waves the slice in my face with a huge grin.

"I love you?"

"Say it like you mean it."

Moms suck. "I love you, Mom. Now get that out of my face

before I blow chunks."

"Ew! Brody!" She laughs and sets the tomato back on the cutting board. "Don't make me lose my appetite."

"Okay. No more barf talk." I smile. "As long as you don't make me eat any of that."

Picking up my bag, I sling it over my shoulder before I head to the fridge to grab something that doesn't taste like a squishy foot.

"Oh, before I forget," Mom says, reaching into her pocket. "You left your phone on the charger again this morning." She slaps it into my open hand while I stuff my face with leftover cake.

"Sorry," I say through the mouthful.

She ignores my lack of healthy taste in food. "I don't know why you even have it if you never use it."

She's right. I use my phone maybe twice a day. Once to turn it to silent, and then again to turn the volume back on. Yeah, I'm that popular.

"Thanks." Kicking the fridge door shut, I give her a fist-bump—'cause Mom's that cool—and slip downstairs to my room.

Oh dude, it stinks. I should've opened my window or something. It smells like morning. You know that smell... B.O., ass, and corn chips. Opening window now.

I plug in my iPod and strip. That ASL room really is too hot. Or maybe it's just me sweating a rainstorm whenever I'm around Quynn. Stupid puberty and shit. Girls don't sweat like this. And if they did, they sure know how to hide it.

In the time it takes to shower and get dressed, morning stank has officially left my room, replaced with cologne and aftershave.

I yank out my homework and slam it on top of my cluttered desk. Homework blows. I asked Quynn once what the point of it all was. She just rolled her eyes and told me to shut up. Then I think I blacked out watching her bend over to pick up all the papers I'd tossed to the floor. Man, that ass.

Whoa! Brody, focus! She's not even here and you're mentally stripping her.

First, Calculus. Better get the tough stuff over with.

Two hours later, Calculus book has a drool stain on it, and

Mom's yelling down the stairs.

"Brody! Answer your phone!"

Huh?

The standard ringtone gets cut off as soon as my fumbling fingers hit the answer button. "Hello?"

"Hey, you got a bunch o' crap at my house. Come get it before Nicole gets here. She needs the room."

Ah, douchebag brother.

"Nicole's moving in?"

"Yeah. So come get your stuff."

"Fine."

Click.

Yeah, I really don't know why I own a phone.

"Yo, Mom!" I call into the kitchen as I tug my shoes on by the door. "Mind if I take the car to Gabe's? I got stuff there he wants me to grab."

"Sure, but *please* don't stay long." The edge to her voice says everything she thinks about my brother right now. "And take your phone!"

"I got it." Door opens. "Be back in a bit." Door closes.

One of these days I'll get my own car, but for right now I have to make a Chevy Corsica look cool. I got my work cut out for me.

Douchebag brother lives about twenty minutes away, but with the way I floor it, I'm there in ten.

My 'crap' is on the porch. At least I don't have to talk to him.

I chuck the box in the trunk and crank up the radio. He makes everything turn to junk.

It starts to rain, and the windshield wipers need to be replaced. I put it on my mental checklist of stuff I gotta tell Mom. Right next to 'no more tomatoes' and 'disowning Gabe'.

Clunk.

Did I hit something? What the hell was that noise?

Thump.

Uh, yeah. Can't be good.

The car slows.

What now?

The car stops.

Dammit. No gas. Wish Mom would've told me it was running on fumes. But at least I didn't just kill a little girl's cat.

The rain picks up—of course—and I hurry and push the car to the side of the road. Please let me have a gas can.

"Brody?"

I whip around. "Hayley?"

Her curvy figure comes into focus as she jogs over. She's carrying an umbrella and balancing a book on her head, her high ponytail holding it in place. I have to blink a few times to make sure I'm not hallucinating.

"Do you need help?"

I raise an eyebrow. "Okay, do you seriously think I'm going to ignore the book on your head?"

She giggles. "The safest place for it is up there. It's a library book, and I don't want it to get wet."

Bizarre girl. Why am I laughing with her?

"Well, I'd offer you a lift, but I'm kind of stranded."

I pop the trunk. Oh good, a gas can.

"How about this…?" She puts the umbrella over my head and takes a step closer. "You let me put my book in your car to stay dry, and I'll walk to a gas station with you so you don't have to look like you've just gone diving in the South Pacific."

I chuckle… again. Dude, what is that?

"Deal." I don't mind getting a little wet, but I don't mind company either.

"Awesomesauce."

Do people actually say that? She grabs the book and chucks it in my trunk before I shut it.

"Okay, you have to hold this 'cause you're taller. I'm not tiring my arm out for you."

Why do I keep laughing at her? It's not like she's being funny. And I'm not normally a nervous laugher. Huh…

"Hello?" She waves the umbrella and the rain splashes down my back.

"Sorry," I say grabbing it from her. "I got this, so you have to hold this." I stick the gas can in her hand. She jerks back when I touch her.

Maybe she's a germ-a-phobe.

"How gentlemanly of you," she jokes. Crap, should I have carried both?

She starts giggling and swinging the gas can as we walk, so I don't feel as bad about it.

"You don't live around here, do you?" I'm horrible at small talk.

"Nah. I was at the library and missed the bus, so I decided to walk to the next stop. I hate waiting."

Duh, Brody. "Guess I should've figured that out on my own, since you were carrying a library book."

She giggles. "I was going to say that, but thought since I don't really know you that well, it would come out all rude and stuff."

She shivers, and I adjust the umbrella, trying to move closer without touching her. "I got a thick skin. You could say anything, and it wouldn't offend me."

"Hmm…" Her eyebrows waggle up and down. "I think I'm going to accept that challenge."

A stupid grin forms on my face. "Go right ahead."

Another laugh. This girl laughs a lot. And makes me laugh too, even though nothing is funny. At least it's not uncomfortable.

"I've never been encouraged to be rude or nosy before," she says.

"Nosy?"

"Well, since I don't really know you, what I'm about to say will not only offend you, but sound like I'm shoving my big face where it doesn't belong."

Whoa, she already has something on her mind? That was quick thinking. "What is it?"

"Nah, I'm not really a rude person. Better keep this comment to myself."

I shrug, trying to make it seem like I don't care, though it's kind of driving me crazy. "Guess you weren't up for the challenge." I grin.

"Guess not." Her face turns toward mine, her mouth in one of those evil smiles that girls do. "And reverse psychology doesn't work on me."

Man, this girl is frustrating. Now I'm uncomfortable and dying to know what kind of stuff she thinks about me.

"Come on, just say it."

"I think I'd feel better if I told you something personal about me before I make a personal assumption about you."

Huh? "Is that an invitation for me to ask you something I don't know about you?"

She nods. "But don't make it something stupid, like what my favorite color is."

"It's yellow." Whoa. That just popped right out.

Her eyes bulge. "How'd you know that?"

I rub my buzzed head with my free hand. "You said it once in class. Well, signed it."

"I did?"

I nod. Why is a discussion over the color yellow such a big deal?

"Huh." She cocks her head to the side as her cheeks flush. "So… pick something you don't know then."

Way to put me on the spot. I'm still trying to figure out what is on her mind. I do pay attention to her in class, and I guess the conversation today is the only one that pops in my head, and I blurt it out before I can think about it.

"You said you don't get asked out a lot."

"Uh-huh…"

"Well, have you ever been on a date?"

"Nope."

Wow, not even a pause. She doesn't even sound disappointed about it. I repeat: bizarre girl.

"Okay, that was pretty personal. Your turn." I nudge her, forgetting her normal reaction to touch until she pulls back, soaking the arm on her jacket. She swipes off the rain drops and tucks back under the umbrella. I really gotta try not to touch her.

Why *am* I touching her?

I clear my throat instead of nudging her to continue.

"Okay, but just warning you," she says, rubbing her fingers across her cheek, "you did ask for it."

"Dude, it must be bad if it comes with a disclaimer." Whatever it is, it can't be worse than having the hots for Quynn...

"I think liking your brother's ex is pretty bad." She says it before I can stop her. "Unless I'm reading things wrong, but I'm an unusually perceptive person."

She's not looking at me, but I can feel the heat coming off her face. Yeah, she's perceptive all right. Or I'm just completely transparent.

"We're here," she says, jerking her head forward.

It's amazing how your feet can lead to you to the right place without a conscious thought. I hand her the umbrella and take the gas can to the attendant, who fills it up in silence.

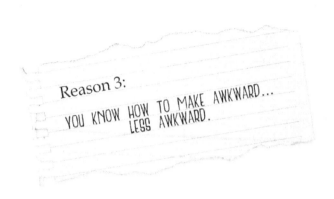

Reason 3:
YOU KNOW HOW TO MAKE AWKWARD LESS AWKWARD.

"I totally messed up, didn't I?" Hayley folds her arms right under her chest, making her cleavage way more noticeable. Did she do that on purpose?

I adjust the umbrella and tighten my grip on the gas can. Yeah, I'm a gentleman the second time around. But still a guy since I just checked out her boobs. "What are you talking about?"

"Well, we were joking around, then my mouth shoots off you're in love with Quynn. I ruined our friendly banter."

She pouts and I have to keep my eyes from wandering down to her chest again.

"You didn't ruin anything." 'Cause, really she didn't. "You just caught me off guard."

"I'm wrong, aren't I?" She drops her arms. Good. I can't really concentrate with cleavage staring me in the face. She slaps her forehead. "Fart, I'm usually right about these things."

I bark out laughing. "Did you really just say *fart*?"

She laughs too. "Yes."

"I thought girls avoided that word around guys."

"We don't avoid the word… just the action."

I have to bend over and set the gas can on the ground so I don't drop it. Seriously, where did this girl come from?

"What?" she asks through pretend offended giggles. "That's my four letter F-word."

After I control myself, I stand upright and grab the gas can again. "I think I like you." Yeah, I just said that. Hopefully she knows what I mean by it.

"Ah, so we're officially friends now because I said 'fart'." Good, she knows what I mean. "That's gotta be the most random and awesome thing ever." She smiles and starts walking. Since I'm slacking on the umbrella covering thing, I guess it doesn't matter if we get wet.

And I'm going to be bold. This girl's easy to talk to and she doesn't seem to judge me too harshly on liking someone out of my league. And who used to date someone who shares the same bloodline as I do. "Well, you weren't wrong."

"Huh?"

"You weren't wrong about Quynn. I'm pretty much screwed."

"Thought so." She doesn't say anything else. And she's not all 'I knew it!' or 'That's so typical' or anything like I thought she'd be.

She's just cool.

"You're not going to tell me to forget about her, or call me a perv?"

"What?" Her eyebrows pull together, and she gets a cute little wrinkle just above her nose. Whoa, did I just think she's cute? Nah, just her expression's cute. She shakes her head a little. "Why would you think that?"

"'Cause that's what normal people would say."

"When have I ever given you the impression I'm normal?"

We laugh… again. Dude. "You've got a point."

"Well, honestly, I don't think it's that big of a deal." She throws me a half smile and a shrug. "I mean, you guys are friends, right?"

"Yeah…"

"And everything between her and Gabe are way over since he jabbed another girl with his pleasure stick, right?"

She just said that. I'm halfway between laughing and shock. "That's one way of putting it."

"See, it's just two single people who like each other. No biggie."

I snort. It's a biggie for me and Quynn. As I said before, it's just... weird. Like she thinks of me as her brother. "You make it sound like it's not against any 'rules' or shit like that."

A slight cringe crosses her face, but it's gone before I can tell if it was actually there. "Well, you're not the only guy who fantasizes about her."

I open my mouth to shoot off a defensive comment about how I hate when people think I'm just the stereotypical horn-dog, but she stops me by nearly shouting.

"BUT, you are the only one who's not, like, nasty about it."

"Huh?"

"Like, guys who just wanna jump her bones look like they're about to smack her butt every time she bends over."

My gut clenches. Maybe I am the stereotypical horn-dog.

"But you're not like that."

"I'm not?"

"No. You look at her more like you care about her. Like you're sorry for what's happened to her, and that your brother was the cause of all the crap she's had to deal with lately. You look at her like she's your friend."

"She is my friend."

"Well, then there you go."

Silence. But it's not crazy awkward. It's kinda nice. I haven't told anyone about my impossible dilemma, thinking anyone in their right mind would call me a creep or a bad brother, and then the word would travel faster than I could take two steps. But here she is, not judging me.

Yeah, I like this girl.

We're at the car, so I dump the gas in the tank, spilling some on my shoes, but they're soaked anyway from the puddles we've had to wade through. Hayley holds the umbrella over my head, and the rain picks up. She has to shout when she talks again.

"Well, thanks for keeping my book dry. Hopefully it stays that way." She laughs.

"D'ya think I'm a jerk or something?" I smirk. "I'm going to give you a ride home."

"Well, I didn't want to assume…"

I shut the gas cover and pop the trunk. She follows me to the back of the car, and I grab her book and toss the gas can back in. I better be a gentleman and open her door. Mom would kill me if she found out I took a girl home and didn't open the door for her. Plus, girls like that stuff, right?

She hands me the umbrella and plops into the front seat. So not graceful or flowery. But like she's a kid about to be taken to Disneyland. I can't help but goofy grin at her.

"Uh, you can shut the door. I'm in, and I'll watch my fingers."

Oh right. Idiot moment. Two seconds later I try to close the stupid umbrella before soaking myself, and toss it in the backseat splashing both me and Hayley with the excess water.

"Whoops. Sorry."

She giggles. "You didn't get my book, so you're off the hook… this time." She pauses. "Hey, that kind of rhymed! Oh, that did too! 'Rhyme' and 'time'. Ha! I'm on a roll."

I wish I could come up with a witty response. You know, something to rhyme with roll. But my mind is still trying to play catch up with this girl's sense of humor. She's definitely weird, but it's not a bad weird.

And now it's been about seven seconds since she's said something, and that's way past the point of making a quip. So now I have to sit here and chuckle like a tongue-tied idiot.

"So, uh… where do you live?"

"Just a few blocks South of Parkrose."

I nod, pull out, and head toward our high school. Her hand goes straight for the radio.

"You don't care do you?" she asks as she smacks the preset stations.

"Depends on what you pick."

"Oh, I know you're a fan of Kesha."

Ugh. "If you make me listen to that pop shit, you're walking the rest of the way." I smile, but it disappears when I see her do that slight cringe again. But she laughs it away. I think I may be going a little nuts.

"Neon Trees?" she asks as she lands on the station playing the band.

"That one's okay."

"Good." She turns up the volume and starts singing along with them. Wow, she's good. And ballsy. I've been on dates before and not once did the girl ever start belting out with the music. Not that this is a date or anything.

The song ends, and she starts flicking through the stations again.

"We're okay, right?"

That came out of nowhere. "Yeah. Why wouldn't we be?"

"I still feel bad about my big mouth."

"You actually made me feel kind of better with it, ya know?"

"Really?"

"Yup. But not like it's going to change anything." I turn on the blinker. "She's way out of my league. And she doesn't think of me like that."

"Hmm…"

My neck pops as I look at her. Her feet are on the dashboard— she's slipped off her shoes and I didn't even notice—and she's tapping to the beat on her knees.

"What?"

"What, what?" She smiles.

"What was that 'hmm' for?"

"Just thinking."

"About…?" I hate when people don't just spit it out. At least *I'm* straight forward.

"Well…" She goes for the radio again. "I told you I'm a perceptive person, and I don't think you're as hopeless as you think you are."

I roll my hand in circles so she elaborates. She laughs.

"Look, I'm good at this kind of stuff—setting people up. Ask any of my guy friends."

"You wanna set me up with my brother's ex?"

She shrugs. "Kind of. Like, if you want some pointers and stuff like that, I think I can help."

Is she for real? Part of me wants to laugh the offer off, stick it in a box and chuck it into the Willamette. But the other part—probably the stupid, hopeful part—wonders if she could really make it happen. Quynn has always been a fantasy. An unattainable source of sexy-ass girl who used to sleep with my brother—which I try not to think about—and a complicated friendship scrunched together in a ball of 'I so wish I could kiss you and not get slapped in the face for it'. But what if she actually became more than that?

"What did you mean when you said I'm not hopeless?"

She finishes singing the chorus to the song. "I think she really likes you too. She just doesn't know it yet." She sings some more. "Or she's holding back 'cause she's not sure how you feel. But I betcha if you play your cards right, when you let loose, she'll be thinking very differently about you, Brody."

Did my stomach just do a little twist? I can't tell if it's because of what she said, or how she said it.

"Turn here. I'm the second house on the right. You can pull into the driveway. My parents work nights." She pauses and laughs. "I'm rhyming again. Geez!"

I put the car in park and reach back for her umbrella. She tightens and recoils against the door when I brush against her arm.

Definite germ-a-phobe.

"Well, thanks for the ride. And let me know about the other thing if you want."

I nod, not sure what else to do. I kind of want to give her a hug or something. But I have no idea why that sudden thought comes to me.

"Uh, y-you're welcome." *You sound like a moron, Brody. Say something else to make you sound less like a moron.* "Maybe next time we talk you'll be rhyming words with 'fart'.

Nice one, dude. Very smooth.

"Start, mart, cart..." She laughs. "Bart, heart, dart, part, tart..."

She laughs again, really loud. "And don't forget shart!"

Her face goes a little red, but I'm not sure if it's 'cause she's embarrassed for saying that, or if it's 'cause we're both cracking up so much the windows fog.

Yup, I don't think it's possible to feel awkward for long around this girl.

She puts the book on her head and opens the umbrella outside the door. "Okay, I'll see you tomorrow, Brody."

There goes that stomach twist again.

"See ya."

Just like that, she's gone, and I'm driving back home, wondering what to do with her offer.

Hayley's good at just about everything she does, so maybe she could help me get the girl.

Am I a lunatic for considering it?

Yes, you are.

But then Quynn pops up. Right there in the forefront of my mind. From the long blonde hair to her flip-flops and I'm there with her, cradling her against my chest and all that other romantic junk too cheesy to share with anyone.

I pretty much blow at getting the girl. I think my longest relationship lasted a week when Lily Peters labeled me as her make-out partner in an attempt to make Ian Dunn jealous. That sucked ass 'cause I actually liked the girl. But oh well.

Since then I've never really been involved with anyone. Few dates here and there, but nothing serious. And Quynn will definitely be looking for something serious. She's a major commitment girl, especially after what happened with Gabe. I kind of want to do that for her. She deserves someone who's not my douche brother. But how do I get her to think I'm for real?

Hayley's offer is sounding better and better. Do I even have her number in my phone? I think she put it in there during one of our classes together, but I can't remember why. And I don't look at my phone often enough to know for sure if she's in my contacts.

"There you are!" Mom says as I trudge in the house. "I told you not to be long."

"I would've been faster if I didn't run out of gas."

Her face goes from annoyance to 'my bad' in two seconds. Dad laughs from the recliner.

"Why didn't you call?" Mom asks, her tone now all gooey, like the one moms use when they wanna say, 'You poor baby!'

"It wasn't a big deal." I shrug and slump into the couch. "Gas station was only about a block away."

"But it was raining." She frowns, and I think she may start stroking my hair or something. Ugh.

"I ran into a friend, and she had an umbrella."

"She?" Dad raises his eyebrow. He's my stepdad, but he's more of a dad than bio-dad is. Bio-dad pulled a Gabe and destroyed Mom's heart by running out on her with another chick. But Mark, he's not like that.

"Yeah. Girl in my ASL class. She walked with me to the gas station then I took her home." Yeah, I'm honest with my parents. Vague, but honest.

"That was nice of her." Mom smiles while Dad still shoots me the eyebrow. "What's her name?"

"Hayley."

"Oh that's right. You're signing partner." Mom waves her hand in the air then sets it on Dad's shoulder. "Well, now that we're all here, we can eat."

She walks off into the kitchen. I'm about to follow her—stomach needs some attention—but Dad leans forward, not looking at me but at where Mom just disappeared.

"All right, kid, I know you're a big boy, but I skipped this conversation with Gabe, and you see how well that turned out."

"What are you talking about?"

"I'd like to think I've taught you by example how to treat the women in your life with respect."

Yeah, he has. So I nod.

"You just be good to all the girls out there."

"She's just a friend, Dad."

"Doesn't matter."

I mentally pat myself on the back for opening Hayley's door for her. "O-kay."

"Are you guys coming?" Mom yells from the kitchen.

I bolt for the table before Dad can unleash anymore parental wisdom on me.

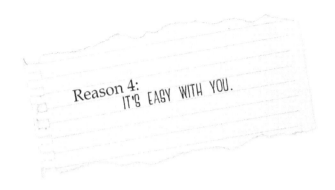

Reason 4: IT'S EASY WITH YOU.

Is this Hayley?
Delete.
Uh, hey. This is Brody. Took you home earlier and I was...
Delete.
So, been thinking about your offer...
Ugh.
This is why I don't use my phone. I sound so stupid via text. I suck in a breath and try again, pressing send before I can change my mind.
Hayley? Brody. Just wanted to make sure I had your number right.
It's gone, and I can't overanalyze my lack of text lingo.
The phone vibrates about fifteen seconds later.
Ding ding ding! You win! Would u like prize behind curtain #1, curtain #2, or curtain #3?
I chuckle and shake my head as I type my response.
2 is my lucky number.
Send.
Okay. Getting easier. Only one try that time.
You've won a 20 min phone convo. with yours truly. Call me when u get this msg to claim ur prize! :)

I hit the dial button before I even think about what I'm doing. She's just easy to talk to. Even via text.

"Sup?" She says it like one of those gangsters.

"Hey."

"How goes it?"

"Uh, all right."

"Wow." She laughs. "You are *full* of conversation. I don't know if twenty minutes will be long enough."

At least she can't see my face go red. "I was just wondering what you were doing tomorrow after school?"

"Hmm… Hang on a sec."

A door slams, and the music in the background muffles.

"Sorry, I think I heard you wrong. Did you ask me what my plans were tomorrow?"

"Uh, yeah." Was that wrong?

"Oh."

Is that all she's going to say?

"Uh, Hayley? You still there?"

"Yeah, sorry. Um, I'm just going to go to the library again, hopefully without the rain this time."

I clear my throat. Why is this so hard? It's not like I'm asking her out.

No, just asking her to hook you up with some other girl.

"Want company?"

"You want to hang out with me?"

"Yeah."

She pauses again. What do I say? Do I say anything? Or just sit here like a moron?

"This isn't a date is it?"

"Uh—"

"Because I don't want your pity."

"What?"

"I don't want a pity date just 'cause I haven't been on one."

I laugh. I don't mean to but it just happens. "No. It's not a date. I wanted to talk to you about, you know, what you said earlier."

24

"Oh!" She laughs. "Yeah, that's totally fine."

"Then I'll pick you up after school. That okay?"

"Awesomesauce."

There's that word again. I chuckle. "Awesomesauce."

"Oh! I gotta go. You can claim the rest of your fifteen minutes some other time."

"All right, see ya."

Click.

Easier than I thought. Even with the semi-weirdness.

***

The student union is always packed during lunch. I don't even know why we have a cafeteria since everyone eats out here anyway.

Sticking my earphones in and turning on my iPod, I get ready for the routine lunch hour: People watching.

Don't know why, but this is what I do. Most of the group I hang out with has B lunch. But lucky me, I get stuck with A.

The music drowns out most of the bull talk, so I try to guess what people say by their body language. The running dialog in my head keeps me entertained.

Jasmine Walters saunters over to Josh, sticking her obviously stuffed chest in his line of sight. Let the commentary begin.

Hi Josh. Don't you just love how big my tits are today?

Yeah, what is it? Two ply?

Why yes! Thank you for noticing. It took me all morning to make sure it was crinkled enough to see.

Good job. Maybe tomorrow you can make them even.

That's a great idea. Why didn't I think of that?

Shaking my head as I chuckle to myself, I turn my attention to other victims of my internal bashing. I spend a few minutes dissecting the theater geeks. They all think they're popular because they're 'Super outgoing!' But really, they're just loud. My music can't even blast their obnoxiousness into oblivion.

Right in the middle of my heckles, Quynn sidles past Brittney, who's doing a ridiculous pantomime. The definition of sexy herself holds a bunch of papers and looks a little like she just came in from a windstorm.

I'm an idiot 'cause I leap to my feet and do a Mission Impossible sprint toward her.

"Hey!" Crap, my voice shakes. I'm supposed to be cool around her. "You need help?"

"Yes!" She grabs the top half of her huge stack of papers and plops it into my arms. "Thank you Brody. I just need to get these to the front office."

"No prob!" Ugh. I sound just as bad as those theater geeks. Note to self: keep mouth shut till Hayley gives pointers.

My stomach twists. Great. Why does this keep happening? Damn nerves.

"Just set them here," Quynn says when we get to the main office. The lights are off, and since we're both buried under papers, they stay that way.

I set the stack down on the already messy desk and they topple to the ground.

"Whoops."

She giggles and balances her stack before bending over.

Don't smack her ass, Brody.

I chuckle at the inside joke I have with Hayley as I lean down to help. "I think it's time they clean off this crap."

She nudges my arm. "I will once finals are over. Two more months." She sighs. "I can't believe it."

Oh yeah, she's an office aide during this hour.

"Mmmhmm." Holy hell. I'm brain dead.

"You going on a senior trip or anything? Last hoorah?"

I shrug. "Hadn't planned on it, but something might come up."

The last of the papers get scooped up and set carefully on the desk. My knees pop as I stand.

"You know, I still have the tickets for Universal."

That's right. Gabe was supposed to take her for Spring Break.

"You still going?"

She twists the end of her ponytail. She does that when she's upset. And it's pathetic I know that. "No. Going would just remind me I was supposed to be there with G-Gabe."

Stupid brother. I wish I could wrap Quynn in my arms right now to comfort her, but my mind quickly comes up with an alternative.

"Sorry," I say and reach for her hand to stroke the back of it. She gives me a squeeze, and my brain shuts off.

"It's fine, really." Another squeeze then she lets go, her cheeks turning pink. "Um, so do you think your parents would want them?"

That would get them out of the house over Spring Break. Sounds like a good idea to me.

"Well, I guess if you're sure you don't want them—"

"Great!" She pulls out her purse behind the desk and digs through it, finally pulling out a couple of creased vacation packages. "Please save me from looking at these every ten seconds."

Why does she have to say stuff like that? It makes me want to smother her in my grasp and hold her till she's put back together. And the other part of me wants to go pummel my jackass brother.

"Thanks." That's all that leaks out my mouth.

"Thank *you*." She plops into the swivel chair. "Really. I'm glad you didn't put up a fight like you did with this." The bracelet I refused to give back to Mom tinkles as she tosses it back in her purse.

I lean against the desk, trying not to knock over any more papers. "That's different. My mom didn't piss you off, did she?"

She pouts and doesn't answer. I grin. I got her there.

"She wants to see you, ya know."

Her forehead crinkles. "I know. I just… can't right now."

"He's never there. Gabe. So you won't run into him if that's what you're worried about."

"It's not."

I reach up to scratch the back of my neck. How can I tell her I want her to be around without sounding like a complete perv? The mom excuse could wear her down. It was worth a shot.

"She misses you." *I miss you.*

A half smile. Okay… getting closer.

"She wants you to come over for dinner." *I want you to come over.*

A full smile and a huff. Maybe one more to break her.

The warning bell rings signaling the end of lunch and the start of fourth period. Damn it.

"I'll think about it, Brody."

I straighten my stance and walk toward the door. "Guess I'll talk to you tomorrow… in ASL, you know."

"Oh! That reminds me." She crosses the room, an arm's length away. Her apple scent fills my nostrils, and I gotta swallow the growing spit in my mouth. "Ms. Stevens said she needed to see you. I was supposed to tell you yesterday, but I forgot."

"Er, okay."

Quynn smiles and blinks. I shake my head trying to free myself from her spell. Before I can mumble anymore incoherencies, I head to class.

Reason 5:
YOU KNOW HOW TO MAKE A GUY FEEL PRETTY GOOD ABOUT HIMSELF.

Turns out I'm about to fail out of sign language. That's fan-shit-tastic. Ms. Stevens gave me a bunch of extra crap to work on and told me to pay more attention to my signing partner 'cause she knows what she's doing. Guess Hayley's not only my 'hook-up' guru… she's now my tutor.

Maybe she'll teach me how to sign 'shove it up your ass'.

"Hey Mom?" I shout from the front door. I toss my backpack in but keep my body outside. "I'm going to the library for a bit. That okay?"

"Yes. Have fun. And take your cell!"

"I got it."

Shutting the door, I pull out my phone to make sure it's on silent. I think that's etiquette for the library.

I've got a text from Hayley. My stomach snarls at me, but I chalk it up to lack of food rather than seeing her name on my phone. Why the hell would that make my gut clench?

Heya. I'm not home yet. Had to wlk cuz my mom 4got 2 get me. But I'll txt u when I get there.

That's not cool. Mom doesn't ever want to pick me up so I just take her car. She doesn't care—most of the time.

I click 'reply' and type as quick as I can, which honestly isn't very fast.

Where r u? I'll come getcha.

Not two seconds later, her text vibrates in my hand. She's good at everything I swear.

Just left school. Don't worry abt it. I don't live far.

I shake my head. **I'll b there in a sec.**

Yeah, she lives a couple blocks away, but it's freaking cold. Not raining, but cold. And she wasn't wearing a jacket today. At least not that I noticed. Not that I was noticing her or anything.

I'm not normally a speeder. Took one ticket and a weeklong grounding to get me out of that habit. But for some odd reason, thirty miles an hour isn't going to cut it, and I barrel toward the school at forty.

Crazy girl thinking she can walk in this stuff and it's no big deal. I get to the school in record time, but I can't find

Hayley anywhere. What route would she take home?

Curving through neighborhoods—faster than I should, but oh well—I finally spot her shivering her ass off. She's huddled over a book, her stuffed bag pulling half her body down, so she looks lopsided.

She's smiling though. Cute.

Gah, there's that word again. *Knock it off, Brody.*

"Hey," I say out my window as I pull up. "Get in."

A wave of relief washes over her face, and my heart does a funky thud-a-thump when she plops into the passenger seat. She smells like mint chocolate brownies and my mouth waters. That's never happened with anyone but Quynn. Weird.

"Okay, I-I know I s-said it wasn't a big deal, b-but oh my gosh, t-thank you." Her teeth chatter.

"Here," I say leaning over and pressing the seat warmer. I'm nearly on top of her before I remember her 'no touch' personality. Her sharp intake of breath is all the signal I need to leap back into my seat.

What's wrong with me?

"Eh…" Crap, idiot moment—again.

She smiles and straps her seatbelt on with shivering fingers, then sticks them under her butt. "Ah," she sighs, "perfect. Thank you."

She's so good at that. Making things less awkward, but my stomach still feels bunched up. Probably 'cause of what we'll be doing today.

I turn on the radio and cock my eyebrow at her. "What's your poison?"

She shivers and shakes her head. "I don't care. Whatever you want to listen to."

I'm not going to mess with it. I draw my hand away from the radio and toward the shifter, trying to look cool as I put the car in drive, flexing my muscles a little more than I would have if I was by myself.

"Holy mother of a trash load."

A large bark of a laugh explodes from my gut. "What?"

"Look at your arms!" She head nods toward them. "You're not like on any sports teams and you're totally muscular."

I try not to look too cocky. Or too flushed either. "Thanks, but I was talking about the mother trash load."

Her face twists in mock anger. "You're just jealous of my lingo. Don't make fun."

"I'm not. I think it's awesomesauce." I smirk.

She pulls a hand out from under her to punch me in the arm. "Shut up!"

Did I like that? Playful punches from Quynn make me feel like I'm about to barf all over her, but Hayley's punch feels like an achievement—like she's finally touching me because she wants to.

A friend punch. That must be it.

"So, did you need to stop by your house?"

"Just for a sec. I'd rather not lug this giant bag around."

"I'm not useless," I say, rolling my eyes toward her. "I can carry it for you."

She laughs. "Trying to make up for yesterday with the gas can, huh?"

"Uh…"

"I'm kidding! But really, I'll be super-fast. You won't even have to get out of the car."

"All right." I go the speed limit this time through the neighborhood and pull into her driveway.

She bends to grab her bag, but I beat her to it, twisting the strap around my palm.

"You're not carrying this anymore. You're going to break your back."

Her hand grasps mine, harder than I would've imagined from her. "It's okay, really. I'll be two seconds. You can stay here."

She attempts a smile, but I'm not buying it. Something's bugging her, but I'm not sure if it's me or not. Should I give in? I mean, it's just a stupid bag. Why do I care if she takes it, or if I do?

"Please?" Her smile twitches as she watches me struggle with my brain.

"Uh, you sure?"

"Two seconds." She unwraps the strap from around my hand and shoulders it. She's out the door and into her house so quick, I have to blink a couple times and shake my head.

Fine. I try to be a nice guy, but girls just have to be stubborn about it. Then they complain chivalry is dead. Screw that.

I rub my hand where she clutched me, the skin full of sparks or something. I shake it trying to get the feeling to go away.

Well, time to go over the checklist I guess. Not sure why I'm still considering talking about Quynn with someone else, let alone actually being pathetic enough to ask for tips on how to make her mine.

Ugh. It *is* pathetic. I should change my mind and tell Hayley to just forget it. We can go to the library and actually... study.

Blah.

I slam my head on the steering wheel, and the horn jolts me back into my seat. Whoops. Hopefully she didn't think I was trying to rush her or anything.

Someone peeks out behind the curtains in her front window as a whole bunch of muffled dog barks shake the glass. It's gotta be her mom. She's older, wearing loads of makeup—it's so bad I can see it from here—and she's got a look on her face like she's about to shoot me with a sniper rifle.

Yeah, I'm not looking at her anymore. The speck on my window is less judgmental. The barks get a little louder for a second, then they muffle again. Before I realize what I'm doing, I get out of the car and open the passenger door like I'm some kind of chauffeur. Hayley turns bright red, but plops down with a small 'thanks'.

At least she doesn't give me shit about doing what guys should be doing.

"Okay," I say as I strap on my seat belt and turn the key. "I… uh…" Brain fart. I know I was planning on saying something, but can't think of it. I retrace my thought pattern as I look at Hayley, but nothing comes to me.

She laughs and flips through the preset stations, ignoring another one of my idiot moments. "No pop. I promise."

There's no conversation between her house and the library. She sings though, to every song that comes on. But I don't care 'cause her voice is kind of hot. All right, not kind of. *Really* hot. And it's taking my mind off Quynn.

I've been to this library once before, with Lily—the make-out partner—and not a whole lot of studying went on. So I didn't really notice how the shelves were set up, or the study tables, or the computers, but I notice now. How can a library be so busy, but look empty at the same time? The computers are all taken, and there are several people sprawled out on couches and bean bag chairs. But there is no one searching the shelves for something to read.

I think they need to rename the place.

Hayley beelines it to the back of the Non-Fiction section, curling up on a couch near some floor to ceiling windows. It's dead to the world back here.

I sit, making sure I don't touch her, and my entire body freezes.

What am I doing?

"It's okay to be nervous." Hayley smiles and tucks her knees closer to her body and rests her chin on them. "It's hard to ask for help, especially when it comes to stuff like this."

"I'm trying to decide if I want to change my mind."

She nods. "Well, I have references." She chuckles, and I sort-of laugh.

"It's not that. This is awkward. Makes me feel like I'm twelve."

"When you used to ask your buddies to see if a girl liked you or not?"

"Yeah."

"Hmm…" She prods her toes with her forefinger and clacks her teeth. I resist asking her what she's thinking about.

"Well, would it be easier for you if I just talked? I'll try not to ask any questions, but give you a run-down of what I think would work in your case."

It's like I'm hiring her to be a matchmaker.

Duh, Brody. That's exactly what you're doing.

I nod unable to come up with anything to say, since my brain is split in two. Quynn… definitely worth this humiliation. But still, it's not exactly how I want to go about it.

"I think the first thing we need to do is make her see you as a guy. Not her ex-boyfriend's brother, but as an available, *single*, guy."

Yeah, good luck with that.

My skepticism must be transparent 'cause she shakes her head, and her voice lowers an octave. "It's not as hard as you think. In fact, easy steps will help."

"Example?"

"For one, you need to call her by her name. Girls love the way their name sounds in a guy's voice."

She's a freaking genius. But I wonder if Quynn'll like the sound of her name being said in a shaky voice.

"Gotcha."

Hayley smiles and relaxes. Guess she's as nervous as I am with the conversation. Mental note: be enthusiastic about her suggestions.

"Speaking of names, you also can't refer to your mom as Mom. That makes it sound like she's her mom too, you know?"

"Good point." I don't want her to think of me as a little brother still. "Should I just use my mom's first name?"

"If you want. 'My mom' works fine too."

I nod, mentally putting it on my checklist of 'stuff I should not say'.

"And you might not want to mention the unspeakable." Her lips pull back as she smiles, revealing her white teeth. I'm surprised a spark doesn't twinkle like on those toothpaste commercials.

"Um... Unspeakable?"

She rolls her hand in the air, like she's waiting for me to read her mind. When I don't say anything, she drops her hand and chuckles under her breath. "Your brother."

Duh. "Oh, right."

"Should I be writing this down for you?"

I give her a face and slouch back into the couch, finally feeling comfortable with the awkwardness. "No 'hey you's', Mom, or Gabe," I say with an arrogant grin. I'm paying attention.

"Ah! A good listener. Something *every* girl wants in a guy. You keep up the good work."

We laugh together, and I have the sudden urge to slide closer to her. I keep my head though... and my distance.

"How do you know all this stuff about my brother and Quynn?"

She shrugs. "I'm observant. It's not like it's a big secret that Gabe pumped it into another girl while he was going out with the hottest girl in our school. That stuff gets around, even though Gabe already graduated."

I nod, hoping that my obsession isn't as well known as everything else about this.

"So, can I be embarrassingly honest?" she asks, cocking her head to the side and looking me straight in the eye.

"I hope you'll always be honest with me." Yeah, that was gag-worthy. Don't know what's wrong with me when I'm around her.

Her face turns pink and her eyes dart to the floor. "Well, I... uh, have like, noticed you for a while. Like how cool you are and crap, so my one major tip would be to be yourself, and not get so nervous around her."

I know there was a helpful bit of advice somewhere in there, but all I can think about is how Hayley has 'noticed' me. 'For a while'. Huh.

"So, like what kind of cool crap are you talking about?" I grin and throw my arm on the back of the couch. Am I flirting? Nah, just being friendly and curious. But her gaze at my position makes me reconsider the movement. I can't shift back right now without looking like a moron.

"Lots of stuff." She shrugs.

"Well…" I start, moving again so it doesn't look like I'm hitting on her. "If you want me to keep doing that 'cool' shit, I kind of need to know what it is."

A tiny cringe goes across her face, and then it's gone. What did I just say? And why does she keep doing that? I couldn't have imagined it… three times now?

Then it hits me.

Shit.

I mean…

"Sorry, you don't like it when I swear, do you?"

Her face goes from pink to dark red so fast, you'd think she was on fire from the inside out. "Um…"

"It's okay. I'll try not to, if it bothers you."

She looks at me dumbfounded. "Really? You don't think I'm a major loser for that stuff bugging me?"

Loser? Hell—heck—she had standards. There's nothing loserish about that.

"Not at all."

The shock disappears from her face and she half smiles. Her big ol' eyes glisten like I've just made her day.

My stomach twists.

"Well, I guess that answers your question," she says.

"What question?"

"That right there is what's so cool about you."

I raise an eyebrow. My brain must be running on slow motion today.

She giggles and pushes my leg—voluntarily touching me.

Stomach twists again.

"You accept people for who they are." She smiles wide again. "Quynn will not know what hit her."

Reason 6:
YOU GIVE THE BEST HUGS.

I don't think I've ever been so nervous and confident all at once. Hayley and I spent the entire afternoon going over the 'simple' things I could do to help Quynn see me as something other than her adopted brother.

I'm skeptical. Okay, that's an understatement. There is no way this stuff is going to change anything, though it makes sense. It's just not enough. Don't girls like big elaborate stuff?

When I asked Hayley, she shook her head like I was asking if Santa existed. "Small and simple things are the most effective. Trust me."

Trust her. She seems to know what she's doing, but still. I want to bolt out the ASL classroom when Quynn walks in.

"All right." Ms. Stevens says from her desk. "No talking today, strictly signing. Turn to your partners, and go at it."

A few kids stifle their laughter, dirty minds at work. I roll my eyes and they land on Hayley, who's also stifling giggles. Great, now my face is red.

So, what should we talk about today? I sign, trying not to picture me and her 'going at it'.

I don't care. You pick.

I glance at Quynn who slides into her chair with a loud huff and slams her book on the desk.

Yikes. Hayley signs as she follows my gaze. *She looks pretty pissed.*

I nod, and force myself to look at Hayley and what she's signing.

I know this is going to sound awful, but this is a good opportunity for you today.

What do you mean?

She smiles and waves me in close. That wave of mint chocolate soaks my nostrils, and I slurp back my drool.

You can…

The rest is way too fast for me to catch. I smile and stop her hands with mine, and mouth, "Slow, please!"

She gives me a 'yikes! I'm sorry' look, then goes much slower with her signs, keeping her fingers close to mine.

You can talk to her after class. See if she'll open up to you.

What am I supposed to say? I've never been good with comforting people. Better at making 'em laugh instead.

I don't know…

Come on, Brody. You'll be fine. You talk to her all the time. And trust me, girls who are that mad, just want to tell someone to get it off their chest.

I look at Quynn again. She's trying to sign to her partner, but it looks like she's holding back tears. I hate seeing her like that. All I want to do is hold her.

Yeah, I guess you're right.

***

"Uh, Quynn?" Using the name. We're alone in the classroom again, everyone bolting home.

"Hmm?" She doesn't look up from her book, her eyes watery and a little red.

"A-are you okay?" Dude, I'm so bad at this. Already my palms sweat rivers.

A puff of air escapes her mouth, blowing her bangs away from her face. "No. Not really."

What do I say now? I glance at the door. Hayley peeks through the window, sticks two fingers toward her eyes then out at Quynn.

Clearly a 'Focus, Brody!' motion.

My eyes flash back to Quynn. She's got her hand over her face, and she's doing some kind of meditative breathing.

"Can I... Do you mind if I ask what happened?"

She drops her hand, finally looking me in the eyes. Her mouth opens and closes a couple times. I wait. Not going to push her if she doesn't want to be pushed.

"Did... did you know G-Gabe is living with... with Nicole?" A fresh wave of tears and hurt rise in her eyes.

Shit.

"Oh dude, I'm sorry." How can I make this okay? I'm not supposed to talk about douchebag brother. "But yeah, I found out the other day. I should've told you."

"No." She shakes her head, a tear finally making its way down her cheek. "It's not your fault I found out the way I did."

"Uh, how did you?" Was that too nosy?

Her mouth twitches at the corner, as if the whole thing is somewhat funny. "You're going to think I'm pathetic."

Doubtful. "I don't think I'll ever think that about you." Whoa, laying on the cheese, but I don't care. I'm being honest.

She half smiles. "Well, I drive by his apartment sometimes. I don't know why I do it, but I find myself down that street a lot."

"That's not pathetic." 'Cause it's not. I do the same thing to... uh, other people. "You saw her there?"

She nods, her mouth back down in a frown.

"Hey," I say, squatting down next her desk so we're kind of eye to eye, "it's going to be hard for a little while. But it'll be okay. I promise."

I know that's so generic, but I mean it. When someone cheats on you, it's going to hurt like hell for a long time, probably the rest of your life.

She nods, and her breath hitches.

This is the part where I should touch her, hug her, or squeeze her hand or something, but I can't. I'm too nervous to do any of that.

Her eyes tear up, and she reaches out and pats my hand. Guess *she's* ballsy enough to touch *me*. "Thank you, Bro."

I nod and give her a dorky half smile as I stand upright. "Uh, no problem. Let me know if you need me. Even if it's just to talk or whatever."

Her eyes flick to the door, and I follow her gaze. Either Hayley left or she's lightning quick ducking down 'cause there's no one in sight.

Before I have the chance to look back at Quynn, she's in my arms, holding tight to my neck and squeezing like she hasn't hugged another human being her whole life and she's been dying to.

She's never touched me like this. Always been those playful touches that didn't mean anything. And I'm trying to feel something about this that makes it feel different than any other time she's touched me, but I can't even hug her back before she jumps away. Her face looks as hot as mine feels.

"Um, thanks again, Bro."

"Uh…" *Think Brody. Find words to say.* "Y-your welcome."

A sigh of relief explodes from her lips before they upturn into a smile. "Okay, well, I've got to head home. Thanks for listening."

"Uh huh."

She goes out the door, and I should've followed her. Should've walked her outside to her car. But I'm frozen in place. Not sure what to think about what just happened. 'Cause if I'm being honest, it wasn't as big a deal as I thought it would be.

***

"So…?" Hayley asks, falling in step with me as we walk down the hallway.

I shrug, still stunned about the unexpected hug. The hug that should've felt different, but didn't. Where did it come from anyway? I didn't do anything really.

"Come on. Tell me. It couldn't have been that bad."

"It wasn't bad." I scratch the back of my neck. "Just surprising." And weird.

Hayley stops and yanks my arm back. "Explain," she says with a wide smile on her face.

"Later," I whisper, leaning in and pointing to all the surrounding people.

She nods and zips her lips, but it doesn't wipe away the smile. My stomach twists a little bit.

"Library today?" she asks.

"How about now? Or do you have to go home first?" Why am I so anxious? I guess I could wait to talk to her about it, but in all honesty, I kind of want to spend time with her. She knows how to relax a situation. And everything in my system is so tense, I'm going to need someone to calm me down.

"I just want to drop off my bag. That okay?"

"Sure, I'm parked out this way." I gesture to the doors down the hall.

When we get to the Corsica, I open the door for her before getting behind the wheel. She's bouncing up and down in the seat.

"Tell me now!"

I laugh and shake my head as I start the car. "It's really nothing, Hayles." It's out before I realize I said it—a nickname. But it fits her. If she's not going to say anything about it, that's what I'm going to call her.

"Nothing, really?" She cocks an eyebrow. "You look like you swallowed a gallon of way hot coffee."

Hayles it is, I guess. "I just talked to her. She was upset about my brother. I know, I know, I wasn't supposed to talk about him, but she brought him up."

"Okay…" She keeps leaning toward me. Dude, she smells real good. I think all girls do. Must be something in their genetic make-up.

"And she hugged me."

She smiles. A big huge one that stretches across her entire face. It's her smile, I'm realizing. "Has she ever hugged you before?"

I shake my head. "Not like that, no."

"EEEP!"

Her exclamation makes me jump in my seat. "You okay there?" I laugh.

CASSIE MAE

"Oh my flying monkeys, this is real good. Small things bring big results. You must've said some serious cheesy crap to make her hug you the way she did. Not that I'm surprised of course."

She talks so fast my mind has to catch up with her.

"Okay, first off... flying monkeys?" I laugh, and she grimaces. "And second, you think it's 'cause I spewed a bunch of sonnets or something?"

She giggles and rolls her eyes. "No. I'm saying you were probably very comforting. So comforting she let her guard down, even if it was just for a second." She pauses as I pull in her driveway. "I told you, you're closer than you think, with her."

Yeah, I guess I am. Either that or Quynn was giving me a 'friend' hug. Maybe that's why it didn't feel like more. But I don't want to think about it that way. It happened too fast for me to overanalyze it.

Hayley sighs before hooking her bag over her shoulder. Before she can freak out on me, I jump out of the car and open the door for her.

"Thanks, but I'll be real quick. Wait here?"

I nod. No point in arguing. That and death-stare mom is looking out the window at us.

Hayley jogs into her house and the drapes swing shut. Some muffled shouting rumbles the window, but is soon covered up by dog barks.

Whoa. What is going on? I kind of want to knock on the door and see if Hayley is all right, but something tells me that would piss her off.

A few minutes later, Hayley comes running out, the dog still yapping its mouth off behind the door she slams in its face.

"Uh, hey. I've got some stuff I gotta do here," she says forcing a smile. Not one of *her* smiles. Her face is a bit splotchy, her eyes puffy red. "Can I take a rain check?"

"Are you okay?" No way am I going to ignore this.

She nods, her fake smile getting wider. "I'm fine. Just have to do some laundry and stuff I promised my mom I would. No big deal."

43

I study her face. Her smile usually goes to her eyes when she's happy. I've noticed, and that's one of the best things about her. But now it's flat.

"Hayley..."

"I'll see you tomorrow?" She looks back at her house, at her mom who's back to staring at us.

"Uh, I guess."

"Hey," she says, grabbing my attention back to her eyes. "A step in the right direction today. At least I think so. You should be happy."

I *should* be happy. But I'm worried as shit right now. There's no nerves or nothing rumbling through me, and I know Hayley hates being touched, but I can't help it. I pull her into my arms and hold her there.

She's so cold, but hugging her freezing skin doesn't bother me. It feels... good. The stomach twists begin as I breathe in her hair. Hot damn! This! This is what a hug with a girl should be like. The stuff in my chest going crazy and noticing everything about the person I'm holding. The curves along her sides, her eyelashes batting against my t-shirt, the fact she's holding her breath, but I'm sucking in her scent like it'll be the last thing I ever smell.

Whoa, what the hell? This is Hayley. Not Quynn.

Hayley.

She hesitates before wrapping her arms around my torso for a split second, then she pushes away, leaving a wide space between us.

"Uh, thanks Hayles." I don't know what I'm thanking her for.

Her cheeks match her red eyes as she says, "No problem. I'm glad the little pointers I gave you are helping."

Huh? Oh, right. She's talking about Quynn.

I nod, and she leaps back into her house before I get another word in.

Reason 7:

I THINK ABOUT YOU
BEFORE I THINK ABOUT HER.

Two hugs. Both I can't get out of my mind. One was so quick I'm not even sure it happened, and the other was…

Amazing.

Incredible.

Confusing.

How can someone get so much from a hug? I can't stop thinking about it.

And she pulled away like I bit her or something. A blast to my ego for sure, but why do I care? Hayles is just a friend.

Just. A. Friend.

It can't be any more than that. I don't really know her, and she's helping me get another girl. A girl I've thought about more than any other girl. A girl who hugged me today too.

Then why can't I stop thinking about Hayley?

I slam my head back into my pillows, toying with the phone in my hand. I've been arguing with myself the majority of the afternoon. Call Hayley? Or leave it alone? Send a text? But that's pretty dick-ish, and I'm freaking worried about her.

My stomach hasn't untwisted since I held her. Maybe talking to her will solve the issue. I've already tried Tums.

In the end, I decide a text is the best solution to ease my

stomach and not pry into her business so much she tells me to get away from her. Though, she'd probably say something more like, "Get the yellow freaking bridge away from me!" Something totally off-the-wall in her cute lingo.

Hey. Wanted 2 kno if ur ok. Call if u can tlk.

I hit send before I have the chance to retype the message eighty times.

I don't know why I expect my phone to vibrate ten seconds after I send the sucker, but it doesn't. It doesn't vibrate for the next ten hours actually. Enough time for me to worry my pants off like a girl.

The five-in-the-morning text goes off just before my alarm clock.

Srry. Didn't get this till just now, & ur prbly asleep. I won't b at school 2day, but I wanna tlk 2 u b4 u go. Call when u can.

'Cause I'm too sleepy to think straight, I hit the call button like the phone will blow up if I don't.

A giggle greets me before she says, "Wow, I didn't expect you to be awake already."

I clear my throat. Okay voice-box, don't make me sound like I'm half asleep. "Uh yeah, early riser." I pause and take a swig of water from the bottle on my nightstand. "So, what's up?"

She laughs again. "You're such a liar. I woke you up, didn't I?"

Thanks voice-box. I'm never asking you to do anything again. "No, I'm just not all the way awake yet."

"Sorry."

"It's okay. I had to get up anyway."

"Well, I just wanted to offer up some advice for today, if you're coherent enough to hear it."

I slide to a sitting position, leaning against the headboard and clicking on the light. Yeah, I think this'll keep me awake enough to listen.

"Shoot."

"Okay, so I was thinking about how much time we've been planning on spending together, and it may give Quynn the wrong idea."

Whoa, wait. "You mean at the library and stuff?"

"That and the rides to and from school."

"Hayles, I've only picked you up twice." I rub my eyes, removing all the crust from the corners. "And besides, I was told to spend more time with you."

There's a long pause when I hear some muffled noise in the background, but I can't put my finger on what it is. When Hayley talks again, she's whispering so soft, I gotta press the phone so far against my ear, I may as well shove the damn thing inside my head.

"Um, why?"

I stifle a yawn before plowing into it. "'Cause I'm falling behind in class, and Ms. Stevens wants me to work on my signs with you."

"Sa-weeet!"

My stomach twists. She's excited to spend more time with me? Why does that make me happy to hear?

"This is perfect," she says quieter, but with no less enthusiasm. "Since I won't be in school today, you can say you had plans to study with me, but I'm sick. And you can ask Quynn to go over some signs after school."

Disappointment soaks my still sleepy body. Right. She's helping me get closer to Quynn.

Quynn.

Quynn.

I wait for a stomach knot, or that normal nervous feeling I get whenever I think about the hot-ass girl I've been drooling over for almost a year, and it eventually smacks me in the chest. Though it takes a lot longer than it used to.

"Uh, I'm not so sure about that."

"Oh my gosh, Brody. You'll be fine."

Major stomach twists now. The way my name sounds in her voice does something weird to my insides. I think I'm going to need more Tums.

"So, why won't you be in school? Are you really sick?" 'Cause she doesn't sound sick.

"Yeah. Got a major headache, so I'm slumming it at home today."

I nod, then remember I'm on the phone. "Uh, yeah. Hope you feel better."

"Thanks." She pauses. "Well, I'm going to go back to bed. Text me though if you need anything. I'll probably be super bored and will need entertainment."

"You got it."

There's another slight pause before she gives me a small, "Uh, okay, bye."

"See ya."

Click.

Is it lame for me to miss her already?

***

"I thought you had ASL down, man," Tanner says after I tell him where I'm headed after the last bell.

"It's nothing. Quynn'll catch me up, if I can find her."

Tanner raises an eyebrow, but doesn't say anything. Even though he's one of my best friends, he doesn't know about the inner crap I deal with when it comes to my brother's ex. For one, Tanner is one of those people who would instantly start going off about her tits. And yeah, I'm not innocent in this area either, but I'd rather not talk about it openly.

"Hey, you're still coming over though, right?" He tosses his backpack on his shoulder and shuts his locker.

Whoops. Forgot about that. "Yeah, but it won't be till later."

"Bring Doritos."

I laugh. "Got it."

"Tanner!"

He whips around with a huge smile on his face. Girlfriend closing in. Time for me to go. Not that I don't like Dani, but I'd rather not be witness to the PDA, which I know is coming. I don't want to be the perv friend who likes to watch.

"Catch ya later," I say.

Tanner gives me a fist bump then turns to close the distance between him and the girl he hasn't seen for a whole two periods. I pick up the pace down the hall when I hear the slurping behind my back. By the time I reach the front office—Quynn was office aide today—my stomach has planted itself firmly in my throat.

Brody, just don't puke on her.

Sucking in a breath—hoping my stomach decides to move back where it's supposed to—I open the door and step into the semi-dark room.

"Uh, Quy—" She's not there.

I get to her desk, searching for her keys or her purse or something, but nothing.

Not sure if I'm relieved or not. My stomach makes its way back behind my bellybutton, but I guess a part of me hoped she'd be here and we'd spend some time together.

Ah well. My signing isn't exactly the best way to impress her.

My phone buzzes in my pocket, and my stomach leaps back into my throat. I texted Hayles every period today, but hadn't got a response. I do a pretty good impression of a twelve-year-old girl when I dig the cell out.

Boo. It's Mom. I mean, Mom's cool and all, but yeah…

"Hey."

"Hi honey," she whispers. I can picture her hovering her hand over the receiver. "I wanted to let you know Quynn is here. I know you see her every other day at school, but still. I know you miss spending time with her."

Hell yeah! "Thanks. I'm on my way home."

I do another impression of a twelve-year-old girl skipping toward the car, and my phone buzzes again.

Hayley.

Hey sry. Been sleepin off the headache. I'm better now tho. R u with Quynn?

No, but I will be. I don't feel like telling her that though. Not sure why.

Nah. She left b4 I could catch her.

That's honest. Instead of starting the car and heading home, I

49

wait for her response. I don't have to wait long. She's fast.

Feel like going 2 the library again? I gotta get outta my house.

Yes. I want to spend time with Hayles too. But how often does Quynn come over for a visit?

Never.

But she'll be there for a while. Probably stay for dinner.

And I'll be at Tanner's. Shoot, what do I do?

Hmm… Quynn'll be talking with Mom. They need time alone and stuff. And Hayles was pretty messed up yesterday. Better see if she's okay.

My stomach twists as I stop talking to myself and type in my reply.

How abt a game night at Tanner's house. U up 4 it?

Reason 8:
YOU SLAUGHTER ME AT GHOST RECON.

"Wow. I think it's been way too long since I've bought Doritos. Look how many different kinds there are!" Hayley taps her thighs to the music playing over the intercom as we walk down the chip aisle.

"Really?"

"MmmHmm." She picks up a bag. "What the fart is Late Night All Nighter Cheeseburger?"

"One of the best kinds." I take the bag and she raises an eyebrow. "What? Not a cheeseburger fan?"

She makes a face. Dude, that eyebrow crinkle gets me every time. "I eat cheeseburgers, just not in powder form on corn chips."

"You're missing out." I put the bag back on the shelf and go for the traditional Nacho Cheese.

"I don't want to be the party pooper," she says reaching for the chips in my hand. "You can get what you want. I'm just a tag-a-long."

I laugh. "Tanner is a Nacho Cheese guy. And you're not tagging along, Hayles. I invited you."

She gives me a wide grin. "Tanner has good taste buds. I like him already."

"You don't know him?" That's a shocker. Tanner's one of those people seems like everyone knows. Football team, popular girlfriend, friends with pretty much everyone 'cause he's so loud.

Hayley shakes her head. "I know *of* him. But I don't know him, know him, you know?" She giggles. "I think I just said 'know' about fifty times."

I laugh... again—always around her, really. "You are so wonderfully bizarre."

Her face gets a little red, and I think mine does too. I guess I said that out loud.

"You haven't seen anything yet." She stops mid-walk right before we get to the checkout stand. "Hmm…"

"What?"

"Want to do something fun?"

Her eyes tell me this is something more embarrassing than fun. "Uh…"

She snatches the bag from my hands and stomps to the cashier. What the hell?

"Excuse me," she says to the lady, who sets down the magazine she was reading. "I was hoping you could help settle an argument."

I've never heard Hayley sound annoyed before. She's always upbeat and funny without being 'theater geek' irritating. Now she sounds pissed.

The cashier's eyebrows shoot to the sky, but she answers, "Okay, hun. What's the problem?"

"You see my friend over there?" Hayley points right at me, and if I wasn't beet red before, I am now. "Well, come here, Brody so you can argue your side too."

Holy hell.

Why am I walking over there?

"Okay, so here's the story," she huffs and turns back to the cashier. "It's my birthday next weekend, right? And Brody here wanted to get some stuff for the party. Now, we've been friends for like *ever*, so he should know I *hate* Nacho Cheese Doritos."

The cashier nods and glances at me. I don't know how I'm supposed to respond. This is pretty much past the point of embarrassing.

"And do you see this?" Hayley grabs the chips and shoves them in the poor woman's face. Now I'm trying not to laugh. "He goes straight for them. Know why?" She doesn't let the cashier answer. "Because they're *his* favorite!"

The chips go flying back on the counter as Hayley turns on me. Her mouth is all about the fake rage over the stupid chips, but her eyes are laughing. "How selfish is that? For *my* birthday, I think I'm okay to request Ranch Doritos. Even though you hate them."

She turns back to the cashier. "Right?"

The poor woman's eyes switch back and forth between the two of us, and she squeaks, "Maybe get both?"

Hayley slams her fist on the counter and both me and cashier victim jump back. "That's not the point!" Her voice cracks. She's crying. *Crying!* Over chips.

Bravo.

I'm a horrible actor, but I'm going to try my best here. This is sort-of fun.

I shove my hand in my pocket and toss the cash on the counter. Taking the bag of chips and Hayley's wrist, I say, "Well, it's my birthday too. We're sharing this party, remember? And if I'm buying, I'm getting what I want."

The look on the cashier's face almost makes me lose it and bust out laughing right there. "You can keep the change."

I tug Hayley toward the door. She yanks from my grasp but follows me. When we get to the car, her face breaks open into a huge smile, and she claps.

"Well played, Brody. Holy freaking baby cows. That was full of awesomesauce!"

I want to grab her in one of those amazing hugs again. This *girl* is full of awesomesauce.

Once we stop our ridiculous laughter, I open the door and ask over the frame as she plops down, "Care to explain why we just freaked out that girl?"

"'Cause it's fun! Also, she was reading the Soap Digest. Thought I'd give her another 'big drama over nothing' story."

She buckles and gestures for me to get in the car.

"You know," I say as I start the engine, "you sure can act. If I wasn't in on it, I would've thought you were really pissed."

She shrugs and presses on the radio, sticking her feet on the dash. "I didn't make up all of it."

"Don't tell me that's actually happened before."

"Ha! No. I was just saying that it really is my birthday next week. Eighteen, baby!"

"Cool. You doing anything?"

She shakes her head, still smiling. "Nah. Birthdays and I don't have the best track record. But still, I'll be an adult! I'm *so* ready to graduate and move out."

Ditto on that one. If I get to graduate, I'm so outta here.

The rest of the drive doesn't take long, and Hayles yaps my ear off about the colleges she wants to go to, whether she'll live in the dorms or rent an apartment, and what kind of jobs she'll apply for. She sounds real excited about it all, making me excited for her, but all this talk makes me wonder if I should get attached so close to the end of the year.

"Okay," she says as we step on Tanner's porch, "you sure he's cool with me being here? I mean, this is a dude's thing, right?"

"Dani's here too. So, no, it's not just a 'dude' thing."

Her hand clasps my wrist, and she tugs me back so I'm inches from her face.

Stomach twists, mouth pools, palms sweat.

Ah hell.

"They don't think… like, this isn't a date, is it?"

Guess the idea of being on a date with me scares the crap out of her.

"Nah, of course not." I gulp. "Just friends hanging out."

She drops my arm and takes a step back, her cheeks flaming.

"Oh good." She sighs. "Then there's no pressure for me to be all flirty and stuff. 'Cause I really don't know how to do that."

Well, whatever she *has* been doing, it's working on me.

I chuckle and walk in without knocking. Hayles gives me a

hesitant look, but follows.

"Doritos?" Tanner pipes up from the couch, not even looking at me or Hayley.

I chuck the bag right at the back of his head. It smacks him and he leaps off the couch, fists raised, but stops when he sees Hayley standing next to me.

"Okay dude, you got lucky. I'm not going to beat you up in front of your girl."

"Oh, I'm not his girl. He only wishes." She nudges my arm.

If she only knew how right she is.

Tanner chuckles. "I like you already. It's Hayley, right?"

She nods.

"Sweet. You can have a seat over there. Dani'll be here—"

"Right now." Tanner's girl skips in, holding a two liter bottle of Cherry Pepsi and smacks a kiss on his lips before turning to face us.

I don't know how people are comfortable with PDA. Ugh.

"Uh, Dani, this is Hayley." I'm so awkward with this. It does feel like a double date now that I think about it. And I know Hayles doesn't want anything to do with that. How do I make this less awkward?

"Sup?" Gangster Hayles has arrived, and she gives Dani a fist bump.

"Yeah, I like you already too. Why don't we hang out in school?" Dani asks as she drags Hayley to the couch. Tanner goes into the kitchen with the soda and chips, and I take a seat on the floor in front of the girls.

"Probably because I'm a major dork." Hayley laughs.

"Whatever," Dani says. "Dorks are the best kind of people."

"Okay suckas! Get ready to be wiped out!" Tanner comes in with a bowl of half-crushed chips, cups, and the soda. He plops them on the coffee table then leaps over to grab all the controllers. I throw Hayley a smile as I lean back to look at her.

"You ever play Ghost Recon?"

She beams at me. "You are so. Going. Down."

***

Sexiness should be based on a scale. And there are certain things that make the points rise or fall. Whooping my butt at a guy's game—not just whooping, but completely wiping me out and rubbing my face in it—yeah, about a million sexy points.

Hayles has broken the sexiness scale.

And my ego, just a little bit. But who cares right now?

"Shit, man." Tanner says, tossing his remote down. "She's good."

There's the flinch but it's gone before I think anyone else notices it. She stands up and victory dances with the controller. "That's right, baby! I warned you, but now you have to eat all that smack talk you gave me!"

Dani starts laughing like crazy and gets up to dance with her. They bump hips and shake their asses as they throw out scores and how girls can 'so beat boys' in video games. I'm pretty sure Tanner and I have lost all concentration. I can't take my eyes off them. It may be a minute before I can stand.

After they finish dancing—thank all that is holy 'cause I'm not sure how much of that I could've taken before I had to leave the room—Hayles plops herself next to me. *Right* next to me. Her warm body presses against my arm and her heavy breath tickles my face as she gives me a big smile.

I have no idea how stupid I look. I think I'm gawking.

"Don't be so sad, Brody. Maybe next time I'll let you live longer than ten minutes."

"Uh, yeah, uh huh." Oh hell, my tongue won't work.

Dani giggles. "You broke his brain! I think that deserves another victory dance."

Yeah, can't handle another one of those. I shoot upright and mumble something about having to piss and get outta there.

Calm down, Brody.

I splash water on my face and dry it off with the hand towel. Why am I so nervous? Even when it comes to Quynn, I never react this way to something so stupid. It's more than just being turned on—which I am—but I can't believe how awesome this girl is.

What is wrong with me? I can't fall for Hayles. She's helping me get another girl. And how screwed up will that be if I turn out to be exactly like douchebag brother?

So make up your mind, Brody. Quynn or Hayley?

I can't believe it's even an option right now. I've spent more time with Hayley over the past two days than I've spent with her period. She's constantly on my mind. Her personality is addictive, not to mention she's hot as hell.

Then there's Quynn. I'm ashamed to admit my initial attraction to her was purely physical. But then I got to know her, and how fun and what a good person she is. She deserves someone way better than Gabe, and though I'm not exactly happy with the way they broke up, I *am* happy she's rid of him.

But am I any better? Here I am with another girl when Quynn's at my house.

Dude, Brody. What have you gotten yourself into?

"Yo, man! Hurry up! I gotta go too." Tanner knocks on the door. I make sure there's no water marks left on my face before I go out.

"Was that hot or what? Dude, invite a girl every time."

He shuts the door before I can respond.

My mind is still so muddied it takes the entire walk down the hallway before I realize the girls are talking—about me.

"Okay, tell me honestly. Do you think Brody is hot or what?"

I'm not an eavesdropper normally, but the question Dani asks Hayles is one I want to know the answer to, too. So I hang out in the hallway.

"He's way hot. Everybody knows that."

Whoa. Stomach twists.

"You guys dating, but not really dating?"

Hayley laughs. "No. We're just friends. I don't think I'm exactly his type."

At least I haven't been obvious.

"Are you sure? He's been flirting with you all night."

Maybe I *have* been obvious.

"Trust me, I'm sure. I know who he likes."

"You?" Dani laughs.

"Ha, ha. No!"

Yes. Hell yes.

"Okay, okay, but let's just say hypothetically, if this girl *was* you, would you go for it?"

I'm leaning forward so much, I have to duck my head back around the wall so they don't catch me listening. She's taking forever to respond! Would she go for it?

"Gosh, I can't even think about that hypothetically."

Why not?

"Why not?"

Thank you, Dani.

"You've seen Brody, right? I mean hello! You know those sexy scales?"

Ah hell…

"Scale from one to ten?"

"Yeah. I'm like a four, and that's only because I've got a big rack. And Brody is like a fifteen. There's no way for me to even contemplate him being interested in me. Because it's just not possible."

Dude, is that really what she thinks? If anything, it's the other way around.

"Just say it *is* possible. Would you go for it?"

"I don't—"

"Hey man, did you get lost?"

Damn Tanner.

"Very funny," I growl as I walk into the game room. Both girls' faces are bright red, and I'm sure mine is too. Tanner seems to be the only one relaxed. But he did just spend a hell of a lot of time in the bathroom.

"Okay, round two, girl. Be prepared for a rematch!" Tanner grabs the controller and sits on the edge of the couch.

Hayles laughs and rolls her eyes. "Your funeral."

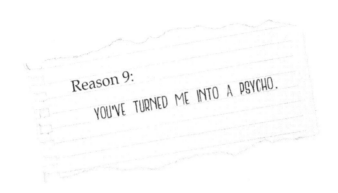

Reason 9:
YOU'VE TURNED ME INTO A PSYCHO.

"Holy super fun! Thanks for bringing me. Your friends are awesomesauce!"

"Uh, yeah. Uh huh." Tongue not working again. Either that or my brain isn't functioning. I can't get her words out of my head, and I wish Tanner would've taken longer in the can.

"Hey, you okay?"

Hayles smiles, but she looks concerned. Can't help but smile with her.

"Yeah, I'm fine. Just tired I guess."

"Okay…"

Silence. Well, not really silence. She sings along to the radio. But her voice is lost in the swirling thoughts going through my head.

I think I want to ask her out. On a date. But she's been so weird about that topic, I'm pretty sure she'll cringe or laugh at me.

And Quynn… well, I'm still not sure how I feel about that.

"Brody?"

Stomach twists. "Yeah?"

"Did something happen with Quynn?"

"Huh?"

Even though it's dark, I still see her face go red. "You've just been quiet. I know I don't know you all that well, but I'm a

REASONS I FELL FOR THE FUNNY FAT FRIEND

perceptive person, remember? So, spill. What's wrong?"

Everything. I'm falling for you, but still like Quynn. Not sure how to ask you out without you freaking on me. Can't decide whether or not I want your help anymore—if I should give up on this whole date the brother's ex thing, or if I should grab you and kiss you right now.

"Nothing."

She clears her throat. "Can I be blunt?"

"Yeah."

"If you're thinking it's hopeless, you're wrong. And you need to stop thinking that right now."

What is she talking about?

"Since I've totally been failing at my pointers today, I'm going to let you in on a secret about girls."

"What's that?"

She smiles. My heart does a funky flip floppy thing. "Hugs usually mean more than just a hug."

"Uh, yeah?"

"Yes."

I get to her street, wishing she didn't live so close to Tanner so I could spend more time with her.

"Hey, would you mind turning your lights off when you pull in? I don't wanna wake anyone up."

I nod, flipping the switch as I park in her driveway. She unbuckles, but I'm not done talking to her. Not yet.

"Uh, Hayles?"

"Yeah?"

"What *do* they mean?" I gulp. "The hugs?"

Her tongue slides over her lips before she talks. Uh, yeah. That's hot. "I guess it depends on the girl, but what I get from it, you said something that made her feel cared for. That means a lot to girls."

"So, it's like a trust thing?"

She smiles and raises her eyebrows. "Wow, Brody. Yes. That's exactly what it is. Quynn trusts you with her feelings. That's huge!"

Right, Quynn. "Uh, can I be honest with you?"

She rolls her eyes. "I hope you'll always be honest with me."

I laugh as she punches me in the arm. Can't tell you how good it is she remembers stuff I said to her before. "Touché."

"Well...?" Her eyes get all wide. I know it's dark, but I'm finally noticing her eye color. Could be just the lack of light, but they are the deepest green I've ever seen.

I clear my throat. *Dude, relax.* "I guess I'm not sure about Quynn anymore."

"What?!" Whoa, her voice can get real loud. "Why? It's only been like a couple days, and you've already made some huge dents. Why're you questioning it now?"

'Cause of you. You're fun, awesome, and hot as hell. And you came out of nowhere, making me feel gooey crap I didn't know I was capable of.

"I dunno."

She shifts, so her torso faces me. I try to keep my eyes away from her chest, but I can't help glancing once. Okay, maybe twice.

"Look, I'm going to ask you plain and simple. What did you feel when she hugged you?"

Nothing.

"I dunno," I say again. "It happened really fast."

"Just think. Close your eyes if you need to. But think hard about what it felt like to have her that close to you—to comfort her."

I do end up closing my eyes. I have to in order to concentrate on Quynn. It was pretty amazing to have her slim and sexy body against mine, even though it was only two seconds. Her arms slung around my neck is what I remember most, and that was hot. I'd always wanted her to hug me like that. Why didn't it feel any different though?

And dude, it was nothing compared to Hayles. Yeah, I was the one to hug her, and it was just as short, but there was something different about it. Her short and cute body snuggled into mine. Her chocolate smell. Her surprise even. And when she wrapped her arms around my torso I'm pretty sure I lost all train of thought.

I could hold Hayles for the rest of my life.

"Brody?"

My eyes shoot open. I almost forgot I wasn't alone.

"Hmm?"

"What did you feel?"

Be honest, Brody. "That I just got an answer I've been looking for." Cheesy, but honest.

She giggles. "Good." Her hand reaches for the door handle. "Hey, what are you up to tomorrow?"

"I don't know. Why?"

Voice-box, do not fail me again. "Do you want to hang out?"

"Oh!" Her face brightens. Damn cute. "Like another game night?"

"If you want." I laugh. "But just you and me this time, if that's all right."

She's so expressive. Her face goes from major excitement to suspicion in a split second. "Not a date though, right?"

I guess not, because that's the deal breaker. "Nah, 'course not."

"Then, yeah! I'm totally up for it. Text me to let me know when I should head over."

"How about I pick you up so you don't have to walk in the rain?"

She shakes her head as she tosses her eyes to the ceiling. "Okay, but don't come in. Like, just text me when you get here, and I'll come out."

Kind of wish I knew why she's so weird about her house, but I don't want to mess this up.

"Great. I'll talk to you tomorrow."

She smiles and steps out of the car—she's got one hell of an ass—and leans back to say, "Catch you later, home-fry."

***

I've got to figure out how to get the corn chip smell out of my room. Not that I'm expecting Hayles to be in my room today—okay, okay, I don't expect, but I'm hoping like crazy we end up here—but it should probably smell better anyway.

I throw open the window, even though it's pouring outside, and start chucking all the laundry on the floor into the basket in the corner. The bed sheets go too, as well as the stuff crammed under the bed. I'm pretty sure there are a thousand empty Monster cans jammed into my overflowing trash.

"Brody!"

"Yeah?"

Mom stumbles downstairs, and her jaw drops. "Are… are you cleaning?"

You'd think I just murdered someone. "Yeah. Got a friend coming over later."

Her brow furrows. "You've never cared before." Then her face splits open with a wide smile. "Is this friend a *girl?*"

Dude. Do not want to talk about this with Mom. But I'm honest. "Yeah. Is that all right?"

"Oh Brody, I don't know…" She bites her bottom lip and takes a few breaths. "I mean, I'd like to be the cool Mom, but I just don't think having a girl here while your dad and I are out is a good idea. Especially if you're cleaning your room. Call me crazy, but it worries me."

Ugh. "She's just a friend."

"Then why are you cleaning your room?"

"Because it stinks."

"Brody…?"

Damn it. She's not going to let this happen. "Look, Mom, Hayley and I are just gonna—"

"Oh! It's Hayley?" She cocks her head, and I nod. "Well, that's fine." She swipes her hand through the air. "I thought… I was assuming it would be… never mind. You kids have fun. I'll be home around ten." She kisses my forehead—ugh—and leaves.

Uh… okay. That was weird. But at least I don't have to worry about Parent Patrol.

I check my phone for the millionth time. Still nothing. I texted Hayles the second I woke up and it's been about four hours. What the hell? Did she forget or something?

Maybe I should just go get her. Tell her I just happen to be in the neighborhood and wondered if she still wanted to hang.

There is something seriously wrong with me. Girl's turned me into a psycho.

I snatch up a pair of gym shorts and toss them in the pile of laundry. Then grab the garbage and trudge upstairs.

Crap. The kitchen and front room are a disaster too. Not nearly as bad as my room, but bad enough I gotta clean it before Hayles gets here. If she gets here.

It's only 2:00. Chill out.

I check my phone again as I pull the front door open.

"Fart! Brody, you scared the poo out of me."

There she is. Drenched to the bone, big smile on her face and a grocery bag in her arms. She scared me too, but I don't let her know. Not sure what comes outta my mouth, but she laughs.

"Can I please come inside, even though I'll drip everywhere?"

"Yes! Get your crazy ass—" She flinches. Oh right. "Sorry. *Butt* in here."

I drop the garbage and run to get her a towel.

"Thanks," she says as I wrap it around her. I kind of want to rub her shoulders and dry her off myself, but I bet she'll slap me if I try. "Lookie what I brought you!" She thrusts the grocery bag in my arms and tugs the towel around her tighter.

I can't help the laugh barreling out my mouth. "Cheeseburger Doritos. Did you give another cashier an interesting story?"

"Nah. But maybe next time." She smiles and wipes a few raindrops from her cheeks.

"Why the he… heck did you walk here?" At least I caught the swear this time. Didn't realize I was so bad at that.

She shrugs and follows me into the kitchen. So much for cleaning everything before she got here. "I like the rain."

"I was going to pick you up. You never answered my texts."

"Yeah, sorry. I don't have my phone on me today."

Her eyes drop to the floor as she sits on the bar stool. Is that all she's going to say about it?

"Uh, am I going to have to ask?"

"Ask what?"

"Why you don't have your phone." I rip the bag of chips open and dump some in a bowl. Guess I didn't have to worry so much about the corn chip smell.

"We're not going to talk about it." Her voice is stern, but she's smiling with her eyes, so I know she's not all that serious.

"Drop it in the toilet or something?"

I could listen to her laugh all day. She shoves my shoulder and rolls her eyes. "No. But it is a bit... waterlogged."

Before I can ask what she means, she grabs a chip, sniffs it, and then jams it in her mouth.

"Okay, so these aren't as bad as I thought. You've got good taste."

"Told you." Laughing, I open the fridge and pull out two cans of Coke and nod to the front room. "You want to play another game?" I'm up for another slaughter, since that was crazy hot.

"Ooh!" She hops off the stool and skips into the next room. "Let's see what you got..."

The small of her back peeks out from her shirt as she crouches. Her wet clothes cling tight to her skin, showing off some serious curves. Going to have to sit down or adjust or something. That is damn sexy. She looks so... soft. Not like bony chicks, but someone who holds their own. If I hold her, I know she won't break.

"Brody?"

"Uh, sorry. What?"

She waves a game in the air by her face, but yeah, I don't know what it is.

"You okay with this one?"

I'm okay with anything right now. "Yup." I put the food down and grab the game from her. She plops on the couch, not even caring she's sitting on some unfolded laundry, and she's still soaking wet.

"Prepare to be annihilated!"

I laugh and just as I pop in the game, the TV shuts off. The X-Box goes out too. I glance at the clock. Blank.

Well, so much for that.

The fizzle of Hayles opening her Coke brings my attention to her again. She's smiling—I like that about her. Nothing gets her down—and she takes a sip before saying, "Guess we get to play something else."

Reason 10:
YOU ARE THE FHE: "FREAKING HOT FRIEND"

"And what is that?" I sit next to her, closer than I would have if it was someone else, but far enough away so I don't touch her.

Damn, she's cute. She tucks her legs under her butt and leans toward me like the idea she has should make me just as excited.

"Twenty questions."

I raise my eyebrows. She wants to play twenty questions? Does she realize how dangerous a game that is?

"You sure?" I say, a smile breaking through. "'Cause you may regret that."

She giggles. "Is that a challenge?"

Competitive. Girl keeps getting hotter and hotter. "Definitely a challenge."

"Okay then, rules."

"There are rules?"

"In my version."

How many people has she played this with?

Don't get jealous, Brody. She's never been on a date, remember?

"Okay…"

"You *have* to answer every question, but you do get one," she holds a finger up, "that you can choose to plead the fifth. But choose wisely. Once you've used it, then that's it!"

That's not so bad. She already knows about Quynn, and besides that, there's really nothing I have to hide.

"Also, twenty questions means twenty total. Ten for you, ten for me. And *any* question counts as one, so if you ask any follow-ups, they count toward your ten."

"Got it." Hope she's ready for this. I'm dying to know more about her.

She adjusts her towel and shivers slightly. I'm such a douche. Girl's probably freezing her ass off.

"Hang on." I fling myself over the back of the couch and race to my room. Sweet, I got a clean sweater and a blanket I can give her. I spray a little cologne on them though 'cause they live in the ass room.

"Here," I say handing her my stuff. "You look freaking cold."

Her face goes a little pink as she smiles. "Thanks." She takes the blanket and wraps it around her, but leaves the sweater untouched. I'm trying not to get a complex about that.

"So, you ready?" she asks.

"Shoot."

She smiles again as she tucks into the blanket. I catch her breathing it in.

Stomach twists.

"Have you kissed Quynn?"

Whoa. She ain't messing around. "Loaded first question."

She shrugs. "Sorry, I didn't mean to cross a line if I did."

"You didn't." I just don't want to talk about Quynn. I want to be with Hayles. "No, I haven't kissed her. On the cheek, maybe, but not like what you mean."

Is that relief in her face?

"Your turn," she says softly.

Since she's going for the kiss question...

"How many people have you kissed?"

She barks out laughing. I give her a 'what the hell is so funny?' look since I can't ask the question out loud.

"Sorry, it's just... I thought you would've figured that already. I haven't been on a date, so, um, never been kissed."

Why does this make me nervous? Why does knowing her lips never touched anyone else's make my abs feel like they've been sucker punched?

I know why. 'Cause *I* want to be the guy who gets to give it to her. Her first kiss, her first date, her first... well, everything.

But hello! That's a lot of pressure. I mean, she's seventeen, almost eighteen. She's waited this long. It better be hotter than hell.

"Okay, my turn," she says, jolting me back to the present. "What do you plan on doing when you graduate?"

Dude. I have no idea.

"I dunno. I guess get a job, try to get into the community college, and move out. That's what I want to do, but not sure if it'll happen."

"Why not?" Her eyebrows crinkle in that damn cute way, and she slaps her forehead. "Craptastic, I just used another question. That's three for me once you answer."

I chuckle and slide a little closer to her. Can't help it. "Well, my grade is slipping in ASL, you know that, but as for moving out? Guess it's 'cause the only place I can afford on a student's pay would be close to my brother, and I want to be as far away from him as possible."

She nods. "Yeah, I get that."

It's quiet for a minute, 'cause really, I'm not sure if she's waiting for me to ask the next question, or if she's thinking. I want to ask her about her family, but something tells me she won't be too happy with that.

She still has her 'veto' though. Maybe I'll give it a shot.

"Uh..." I clear my throat. *Dude, Brody, just get it over with.* "Why don't you ever want me to walk you to your door?" That's an innocent question, right?

"Because it's not a big deal." She smiles, but it doesn't go up to her eyes.

"Is there a rule about lying? Because there should be."

Her eyebrows shoot up, and she smiles all the way. "I've never been good at lying." She laughs. "The truth? I don't want you to meet my mom."

I don't care about the follow up question taking up one of mine. Gotta know. "Why?"

"Okay, that's question three for you. And that's the one you're not getting an answer for. My turn."

"But—"

"Are you a virgin?"

Way to take my mind completely off its train of thought. She's good.

"Uh, yeah."

It doesn't bug me I'm still a virgin. At least not with her, since she hasn't even kissed someone, but still, for an eighteen-year-old guy, it's hard to admit out loud.

"Hey! Me too!" She laughs and kicks me in the shin. I wish she'd keep her foot there. I can't believe this girl hasn't been on one date. It has to be due to her and not for lack of options.

I want to ask her out. Not just to 'hang', but to hold her hand and open her door and all that other stuff that goes with it. But I can't do that without feeling like she'd get all weird on me.

We are playing twenty questions though...

I take a deep breath and go for it. "If I asked you out, what would you say?"

She rolls her eyes. "Knock it off, Brody."

"That's what you'd say?"

"No, I'm saying choose another question."

"Why?"

"Because you have to ask something that's not completely crazy. Something *real*."

"You think it's crazy that I'd want to ask you out?"

"Yes."

"Okay, why?" I stop, trying to count back how many questions that was, but I don't really care. "And that only counts as one question since you didn't answer me."

She tugs the blanket around her, taking another breath of it.

"So, you want to know why I think it's crazy that you'd ask me out?"

"Yup."

She pauses, her eyes going to the ceiling, down to the floor, over at the TV. This girl is killing me.

"It's a long answer. You ready for it?"

"Yeah." Hell yeah. Maybe then I'll know how to convince her how crazy *she* is.

"First, I know who you'd really like to go out with, and it's not me."

She's really wrong about that one.

"Second, we've hung out like, what? Three times? I'm actually surprised you haven't ditched me already with how weird I am."

That's one of the best things about her.

"Third—and you're going to hate this reason, but it's true— look at me."

Oh, I have been.

"I'm not exactly Miss Size Zero."

Huh?

"I'm what they call the FFF."

"Meaning?"

"The Funny Fat Friend."

What the hell? I know she's going to get self-conscious, but I look her over. I mean, I've been checking her out for the past couple of days. Never once did it cross my mind that she's fat. Girls say that all the time, but the way Hayles said it, it's like she actually believes it and she's all right with it.

Maybe that's why she doesn't care when people moo at her.

I wouldn't call her fat though. She looks like an hourglass. Big in the *right* places. And that stuff doesn't matter to me anyway. This girl is amazing.

"Hayles—"

"You don't have to say it, Brody."

"Say what?"

"That I'm not fat. I know you feel you have to, but you don't. Really, I'm okay with it." She adjusts on the couch, crossing her arms

71

and the blanket around her stomach. Trying to hide it or something.

"But—"

"Please." Her voice cracks. Dude, I was going to tell her I think she's damn sexy, but now I'm not sure if she'll want to hear it.

I scoot closer again. She doesn't shift away, so I take a stab at telling her what I think of her.

"You know, I don't know many of your friends, but I'm pretty sure you're the hot one." It's a round about way of telling her she needs to realize how freaking beautiful she is.

Her cheeks flush, and she smiles as she rolls her eyes. "Yeah. O-kay." She shoves my arm, but her hand lingers there, playing with the fabric of my shirt.

Damn, that feels good. Gut is getting all crazy twisted again. I want to grab her hand and hold it there.

Then her breath catches, and she snaps her hand back under the blanket. Her face gets dark red, and she avoids eye contact with me.

"Well, given the fact all my friends have boyfriends and I have yet to go on a date, I'm pretty sure I'm the FFF, but whatever."

She's trying to change the subject. Did I make her that flustered? Nice.

"It's probably 'cause you were the one to set them up. You said that right?"

"Yes, I did. Freaky Frisbees, you *are* a good listener."

When it comes to you, hell yeah. "So, question like six or something, how did you get into that whole deal?"

Her face falls, and her eyes go straight to the floor.

"Crap. I already used my 'no answer'." She sighs. What is so bad? Guess the right thing to do would be to let her off the hook and tell her not to answer, but too bad. I'm going to do the wrong thing and make her answer. I gotta know more about her. It's like a freaking drug. And the more I find out, the more I want her. I'm almost sitting on top of her now that I think about it.

"Yup, you did. So whenever you're ready…" I smirk and her cheeks go pink again.

"It's another long answer."

My eyes flick to the window. It's still pouring like snot out there. "Looks like we've got time."

"Okay, so there was this guy. Jason."

"Dolley?"

"Yeah."

I know him. He's one of those punkers who think they're real good at the guitar, but really, they blow.

"Anyways, when I started high school, me and my girlfriends went out and met up with a few boys. One of the guys was Jason and he like, was way cute and nice to me and asked for my number at the end of the night."

"I thought you said you hadn't been on a date." I smile and cock an eyebrow. I want to touch her, but I keep my hands to myself.

"I don't count that as a date 'cause it wasn't. Just a group of friends hanging out."

"But he asked for your number. That sounds like he was into you."

I shouldn't be jealous of something that was forever ago, but I am. Stupid punk dick.

"Right? I knew I wasn't crazy about that!"

"Huh?"

"Well, he asked for my number and called me... a lot! Like every freaking day. I thought, 'Holy crap! Someone actually picked me out of all my skinny gorgeous friends. Score!' But, then after a couple of weeks, he asked if we could all hang out again. As a group, which I was okay with. You know, less pressure and crap."

"Okay...?" Yeah, still not getting where this is going.

"Well, he asked if Lexi would be there. I told him yes, 'cause she's like my best friend, and he asked me... well, he asked if I could talk him up so he'd have a chance with her."

What a pussy. Even in the ninth grade, I knew how to ask out a girl without going through the best friend first.

"Well, I was a little pissed, and a lot hurt, but I probably just read things wrong."

"No—"

"But when I told Lexi about Jason, she was so thrilled… I guess she was into him too, so I set them up."

"Wait, she didn't know you liked him?"

"No. I don't tell people about my crushes. It's like voicing them only makes it worse when they don't like me back."

That makes sense. But dude, still feel like kicking Jason's ass until my foot pops out his mouth.

"They still together?"

"Yeah." She scratches her nose and slides closer to me. Damn. Her wet hair mixed with her normal chocolate smell is a real turn on. "The same thing happened with Mike, Wes, and Nick. That's when I learned not to get my hopes up with every guy who paid me even the smallest amount of attention. To take matters in my own hands, and offer to help out before I could get hurt… or attached."

Shit.

Shit. Shit. Shit.

I'm no better than any of the other douchebags who used her to get to someone else. It may have started that way with me, but it sure as hell won't end that way.

No wonder she's so weird about dating.

"Anyway, all my friends now have boyfriends I set them up with. And I'm pretty good at it, since they are all still together." She smiles and pats my leg. "So there's my resume! Do I have you convinced now I can get you with Quynn?"

I nod, but I'm not really paying attention anymore. I feel like shit. She's never going to think I'm for real until I tell her Quynn isn't who I want anymore.

It's her.

But will she ever believe that?

"So, I've lost count on our questions." She laughs, her breath tickling my face. "But I'm pretty sure you've run out."

I nod.

"Hey."

I look at her.

"You okay?"

No. I'm not okay. I've got a girl who refuses to believe anyone could fall for her because she's fat, and she refuses to fall for anyone else because she doesn't want to get hurt.

I don't ever want to hurt her. I want to be with her. Hold her and show her she's freaking wrong.

"Yeah, I'm fine."

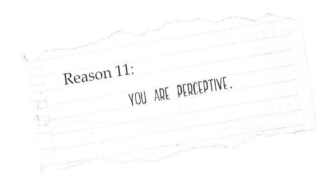

Reason 11:
YOU ARE PERCEPTIVE.

One day. One damn day since I talked with Hayles. I've never been more happy for a Monday.

Funny thing, it's not 'cause of Quynn that I'm anxious to get to the ASL room. I have the palm sweats and the gut knots and all that other stuff that tells me I'm in way over my head. That's normal for the ASL room, but it's for a different girl this time.

And it's about a hundred times worse.

I kind of wonder if it's 'cause I couldn't text Hayles at all after I dropped her off. I really regret not asking her more about her 'waterlogged' phone. I'm asking today 'cause this shit sucks. It's like I *need* to talk to her. All. The. Time.

Damn it.

I *am* in way over my head.

And it's only lunch time. Just one. More. Hour.

I jam my earphones in and crank up the music. I'm not in the mood to people watch today. Gotta calm my nerves.

I'm going to do it today. I'm going to ask her out, and she's going to say yes and believe me. Even if I have to freaking shake her until she gets it.

Drumming my fingers on my knees, I close my eyes and try to erase everything twisting in my stomach. It's just a girl. Just a girl.

Done this before. What's the worst that can happen?

She'll say no.

Then convince her to say yes.

Good luck with that, Brody. She's pretty firm on her self-image.

Well, she's wrong.

One of my earphones gets pulled out and my eyes snap open.

"What are you listening to, homie?"

Can't help feeling like I may hurl all over her as she sits down—right next to me again—and sticks the headphone in her ear. I go to turn it down, but she stops my hand, keeping hers on mine as she listens.

Can't. Concentrate.

She's all warm and soft and crap. I want to grab her into my arms and keep her there forever.

"Mr. Grant, I've underestimated you."

"Huh?" Yeah, I'm going to try to ignore the fact it doesn't matter what name she calls me, I like it. Point for Hayles about the name thing.

"You have good taste in more than just chips." She grabs the iPod out of my hand. Her finger flicks through the playlists, and I hear a small, "Ooh!" before the song changes. Then she hums along softly by my face.

Damn beautiful.

"Uh, Hayles?"

"Mmm?" She turns the music down.

Bailing… "I didn't know you had this lunch."

"Yup. Right now you're saving me from the slob fest going on in the cafeteria." Her eyes toss up to the ceiling before meeting mine. "I *hate* being witness to PDA."

I chuckle. "Yeah. I know the feeling."

"Tanner and Dani?" She smiles and winks.

"Uh huh." I pause and nod toward a couple of Hipsters going at each other across the hallway. "But they're not as bad as that I guess."

Hayles follows my gaze and shivers. "Gag me."

She goes to turn the music back up, but I stop her. Hell yeah! She lets me keep my hand on hers.

All right, Brody. Just ask her out. Not a big deal.

"Hey, uh… so I was wondering—"

Bell rings.

Damn it.

She grins, tossing my earphone in my lap. "Tell me on the way to class."

Can't do it. Not on our way to the class we share with Quynn. Not in the middle of a chaotic hallway in this craphole we call high school. I mean, she's never been asked out before. Well, I assume she's never been asked. That's what she said, right?

More pressure to make this good for her. She deserves that.

"Brody?"

"Huh?"

"Are you mad at me or something?"

Guess we've been walking to class, and I haven't said a word. Didn't even notice.

"No." I attempt a smirk, but it probably looks real stupid.

Her brow crinkles in that hot way it always does, and she points a finger at me. "Well, something's bugging you. You're a lot quieter than normal. I mean you're usually quiet, but today you seem…"

"In a daze?" My smirk is for real this time.

She smacks her forehead. It's so cute when she does that. "Gosh dang gorillas, I'm such an idiot."

My eyebrow pulls upward. What is she on about now? "Because…?"

"Because I know why you're quiet and I should've figured it out by now."

Huh? Am I that transparent?

"Don't be nervous about seeing her today. Maybe ask for some help after class. Like, totally botch it with me or something." She giggles and it takes me a minute to catch up with her.

Right.

Quynn.

Signing.

Pointers.

I don't want to think about all that crap—the mess I've made already with everything. And I know Quynn'll ask why I wasn't home on Friday when she came over.

Hayles is going to be pissed when she finds out.

Or maybe it'll be enough to convince her I'd rather be with her than Quynn. May work in my favor.

Maybe *I'll* bring it up.

"Hey." She stops in front of me and grabs my shoulders. I flex underneath her grasp, showing off.

Her face goes a little pink, but she keeps her hands on me. "It's no different than it was before, okay? Don't be nervous. You've got this in the bag."

I open my mouth to pretty much tell her everything, but she stops me.

"And I'll tell you another secret." She drops her hands and gives me a faint smile. "She looks at you the same way you look at her. She… she really likes you. She's just waiting for the right moment."

I'm as big a douche as my brother, because I don't care.

I don't care.

It's not the right girl. A week ago, maybe, but now? Man, I just want Hayles.

"Hey," I say as I snatch one of her hands and play with her fingers. That feels good. She's not pulling back either. "I'm not nervous about Quynn. I told you, I'm not really… I'm not sure about her anymore."

She gives me a 'whatever' look and pulls her hand away.

"Knock it off, Brody."

***

Quynn's wearing her same old sweater and jeans, but her hair is down today. I know this means she's in a good mood, and it pisses me off that I know that.

And it shouldn't make me want to brush it from her face, but it does. Ugh. Thought I was over this girl.

Hayles waves her hand in front of my face and brings me back into her view.

Whoops, should be paying attention. Especially to the girl I actually want.

What are we going to talk about?

She smiles and my stomach twists.

I have a question for you.

It's going to suck asking her like this, but I don't care. Maybe rejection will be better in sign language.

More questions? I believe you ran out on Saturday.

I smirk. *Okay, so you've got some for me, then?* I'm stalling—again, but I don't care. I like our banter. It's so... easy.

I totally just dug myself in a hole. Now I can't think of anything to ask you. She laughs under her breath as she swipes her bangs from her face.

You forfeit one of your questions to me, then?

Her nose scrunches as she gives me a look that's so damn sexy, it's hard for me not to close the distance between us. Even in front of everyone. In front of Quynn.

Man, I got it bad.

Fine. What's your question?

I throw a quick glance at Quynn. Her eyes dart from mine and shoot to her signing partner. Her face goes bright red. Was she staring at me? Listening to our conversation?

Damn it. I *can't* do this in front of her. She won't get it. Hayles isn't like other girls. Hell, she doesn't even understand why anyone would like her. Why would Quynn?

Chickening out again. And now I got to come up with another question.

What do you want for your birthday?

Hell yeah! I came up with that pretty quick.

She taps her chin with her forefinger and looks up at the ceiling. Even this gets me going.

I'm screwed.

Don't laugh?

I cross my heart and salute. She giggles.

I want a tattoo so bad!

Why the hell would I laugh at that? I smile and remove my leather wristband, showing her the tatt I got on my eighteenth birthday.

"Sweet!" she whispers as she grabs my wrist and traces her fingers over the ink. The soft touch sends goose bumps up my arms, and I kind of hope she notices. Maybe she'll get the hint I've fallen for her.

She lets go to sign to me.

What does it mean?

Kind of knew she'd ask me that, but I don't want to tell her here. Not with Quynn sitting two feet away. I wrap the leather back around my wrist.

Later?

She nods.

You figure out a question, yet? Or do I get another one?

Her eyes get wide, and she leans toward me. Yeah, she gets closer every time we talk now. That chocolate smell will be burned into my nostrils. I'm okay with that.

You have more? Gosh, Brody, didn't realize you wanted to know so much about me.

I want to know *everything* about her. I don't even care how cheesy that sounds.

You got your phone yet? I wink, and she shoves my arm.

No. Still getting it fixed.

You going to tell me what happened?

It's like I asked her to boil puppies or something. Her face gets all twisted for a second, then she wipes it clean with a fake smile.

Nothing. Just got it wet.

She's lying. Or at least not telling the entire truth. Part of me is kind of happy I know this about her already, but the other part is mad she doesn't feel like she can tell me stuff.

Stupid, I know. It's just a phone.

You seem pissed today. Her hands sign it real fast, but I catch it. *Are*

REASONS I FELL FOR THE FUNNY FAT FRIEND

you sure you're okay?

Not pissed. Nervous. Never felt it this bad before. Look at what she's done to me!

I'm fine, Hayles. I promise.

She cocks her eyebrow and nibbles the inside of her lip, but drops it.

Okay. You going to be busy after school? Her eyes flick to Quynn, who again goes pink and looks at something that became very interesting on the ceiling. Hayles stifles a giggle. *Looks like someone wants to talk to you.*

Yeah, it does look that way. Probably about Friday, or more about douchebag brother. I don't really want to deal with that right now.

Hayles. That's what I want to deal with.

Did you want to hang out again today?

She shakes her head. *I was only asking to see if you were going to talk to Quynn after class.*

Wasn't planning on it.

Her face scrunches up. *Why not?*

'Cause I want to be with you. *Thought maybe we could hit the library again.*

You'll tell me about your tattoo? Her eyes get all excited as she waits for me to answer her.

How can I say no to that?

Yeah.

Sounds good.

Definitely sounds good.

***

"Brody? Could I talk to you for a minute?"

Quynn's voice is all shaky, but she looks confident as she perches herself on top of my desk again.

Hayles smirks at me as she swings her heavy bag over her shoulder.

"Hey, wait for me, okay?" I ask.

Her eyebrows shoot upward, and she opens her mouth, looking

82

like she wants to argue, but I give her a look. She shuts it and nods before walking out the door.

Deep breath.

"Sup?"

"Bro," she says before grinning, "you've never said that before. Who've you been hanging out with?"

I chuckle, but don't respond other than that. Kind of want to get this over with. Half 'cause Hayles is waiting for me, and half 'cause I'm not sure if the stomach twisting is because of Quynn or Hayles, and I don't want to be more confused than I already am.

"I went to your house on Friday."

I clear my throat. "Uh, yeah. My mom told me about that."

She smiles. "Thank you for talking me into it. I can't remember the last time I was able to enjoy a Friday night."

Good, she's not mad. Maybe I was reading too much into that sort-of hug she gave me last week. "No prob." I twist the strap of my backpack around my wrist and stand. "That all you needed?"

"Oh!" Her face goes red, and she dumps my books off the desk with her hip. "Um, no. I wanted to talk to you about something else too." She bends to pick up the books, and I'm not as big a douche as I thought 'cause I help.

"Shoot." Wish she'd just spit it out. Hayles is waiting for me.

Her face gets red again as she hands me my stuff. "Just wanted to know how things are going with your signs. Your mom said you were having trouble."

I shrug. "Good. Hayley's helping me out. Think I'll be okay."

Half smile. "Oh, well… I thought… if you want…" She pauses for a second, clacking her tongue and looking at the door. "I don't mind going over signs with you after school. That is, if you don't feel weird about that."

Damn it. Opportunity I've been waiting for, and now I don't want it.

"Uh, thanks. But I'll keep trying with Hayley for a bit."

"Okay. Just let me know if you ever need my help."

"Yup." Gotta get outta here. Starting to get awkward. I walk toward the door, but her voice stops me again.

"Hey, Bro?"

"Yeah?"

She takes a deep breath and twirls her hair in her hand. Damn it, she's got something on her mind. I'm trying not to care, but it's hard.

"Something wrong?"

Half smile—again. "Well, I have plans to stop by and see your mom on Friday again. I was kind of hoping I'd see you too for a bit. Like before, you know?"

Friday. Hayles' birthday. If I ever get the guts to ask her out, and she says yes, I won't be home. At least, not long enough to hang out with Quynn like we used to. There goes my freaking luck, choosing between two amazing girls.

The choice is easy though. Surprisingly easy.

"Maybe. I may have plans though."

"Oh?"

"Yeah."

I should say it. I should say it right now. *I'm going to take Hayles out.* But I don't. I can't find the words. I don't want to find the words. Not sure if Quynn would understand. Hayles isn't... it's just different.

"Okay, then. I guess I'll see you next class." She's sad, and I hate it. But I can't do anything about it. Not without screwing things up.

"Later." I smile, trying to seem like this isn't the most awkward conversation I've had in my life.

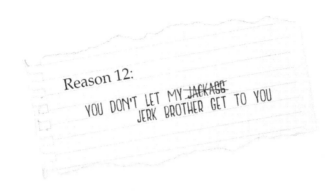

Reason 12:
YOU DON'T LET MY ~~JACKASS~~ JERK BROTHER GET TO YOU

"Sorry. I just want to drop off some stuff," I say to Hayles as we pull in my driveway. "You want to wait here?"

"Heck no!" She smiles as she unbuckles. "I want me some Coke, if you got any."

I laugh and quickly grab the door for her. "Sure."

She's bouncing as we walk up the porch. It's going to be a good afternoon, I can tell already. I don't want to ruin it by asking her out, but I'm going to. Just have to find the right moment.

I stick the key in the door and step back to let her in first. She brushes past me and I have the sudden urge to touch the small of her back. Just to rest my hand there. Dude, I want any excuse to touch her at all.

She stops in the entryway and I sidle up next to her, 'accidentally' bumping into her back. She doesn't move, which surprises and excites me—for about two seconds.

"Damn, dude. Don't mind me. Just forget I'm even here."

Douchebag brother.

"What the he—" Oh right, Hayles is here. "Heck are you doing here?"

Gabe stalks to the fridge, his ass sticking out of his jeans. He's wearing boxer briefs, but still doesn't leave much to the imagination.

Hayles averts her eyes, like the red wall by the stairs is the most interesting piece of artwork she's ever seen.

"I'm outta food."

"Go buy some then."

"Can't." He swings open the fridge and pulls up his jeans, which fall right back down. "Nicole don't get paid till the thirtieth."

"Get a job."

He chuckles and smacks a brick of cheese, mayo, and jar of pickles on the counter. "That's why I have Nicole. So I don't *need* a job."

"And here you are stealing food from your mom."

I don't give a shit he's waiting on his suga momma. He needs to get the hell outta here before I lose it in front of Hayles. Just looking at the prick makes me want to punch the crap out of him.

"Touché, little bro." His idiotic laughter gets muffled as he sticks his head in the cupboard.

"Um," Hayles whispers in my ear. "Bathroom?"

Yeah, I don't blame her. "Down the hall, second door on the right."

"Thanks."

She's gone, and I'm storming into the kitchen. I fight Gabe as he takes things out, and I put them back.

"Dude, chill!"

"You need to get out!"

"Geez, who pissed in your lunch?" He grabs a grocery bag from under the sink and starts shoving as much food as he can into it. "I told you to forget I was here."

"You can't just pop in after ten months of nothing but being a complete dick to Mom and Dad. Then there's Quynn—"

"Oh, I get it." He pulls up his jeans, which again does no good. "You still into my ex?"

I gulp. "What are ya talking about?"

"You know what I'm talking about. I don't blame you, kid. She's damn sexy. Piece o' work, but she was good in the sack. I say have a go at her if you can. But don't be pissed at me for moving on to richer fish."

Can't take this anymore. I slam him against the fridge, holding him by his stupid-ass Korn shirt. "You better shut your mouth before I do it for you."

He chuckles, and I tighten my grip.

"It's not funny, dickwad."

"All right, all right." He shakes from my hold, and I reluctantly let go. If it wasn't for Hayles in the next room, I'd beat the crap out of him.

He digs through more cupboards and I let him. I just want him out of here.

"Bingo." He pulls out Dad's six pack of Corona. I know I'm going to get an earful from Dad, but I don't care.

"Look little bro," Gabe says, getting all his 'hard-earned' food together, "learn from my damn shit and don't get attached too young just 'cause your girlfriend's got one hell of an ass. Bang any chick who'll give you whatever you want without nagging your balls off. And mooch off your parents when they aren't home. Trust me, this shit's a lot easier than working your ass off for minimum wage."

He opens a beer and slides it across the bar to me, then opens one for himself. "Oh, and stop being so damn pissed all the time."

He slugs me in the arm as he passes me, beer in one hand, bag of half the food from our fridge in the other.

I'm not sure how he became such a dick. But if it's genetic, I hope it bypassed me.

"Get out." I don't touch the beer, though I kind of want to once he leaves.

He stops at the door to give me one of those stupid cocky smirks. "Have fun with your girl. Didn't peg you as a chubby chaser, but whatever gets you action. Might help with your attitude."

If I was faster, he'd have a broken face. But he's gone before I can get to the door.

"Well," Hayles says from the hallway. Oh crap, please tell me she didn't hear that. "He's a real charmer." She smiles, but her eyes are filled to the brim with tears.

Crap. Crap. Crap.

"Hey," I say, closing the distance between us. I don't care how awkward this may be or that she hates it when I touch her. "Don't listen to him, all right? He's a jacka… he's just a jerk."

She nods, attempts another smile and shrugs. "No biggie. I stopped listening after the nagging balls comment."

She's lying, but how do I make her feel better without making this worse? I go to wrap her in a hug, but she coughs and takes a step back.

"Do you mind if I use your phone?" she asks. "I wanna check and see if mine is ready yet."

"Sure." I tug my phone outta my pocket and slide it into her open palm, ignoring how moronic I feel for trying to comfort her and failing.

"Thanks dawg. I'll just be a sec." Another fake smile.

I nod as she presses the phone to her ear and turns around. Better give her privacy, even though I want to wrap her in my arms and apologize over and over for my dick of a brother. Stalking to the kitchen, I grab my backpack I dropped by the door and start putting away the mess Gabe made. Dad's going to kill me for letting him take his favorite beer, but nothing I can do about it now.

After putting the bread loaf douchebag brother took half of away, I glance at the clock on the microwave.

Where is Mom? She's usually home by now. Actually, she should've been home an hour ago.

Maybe she saw Gabe and took off running while she could. Mom is one smart lady.

A long sigh escapes Hayles mouth as she walks in the kitchen.

"Favor?"

"Sure. What's up?"

She slides my phone across the bar. "My phone's all fixed. Mind taking me to *Verizon* to pick it up?"

I smirk. "Only if you tell me how it got waterlogged in the first place."

A giggle and an eye roll is the only answer I get.

"All right." Stubborn girl. "Let me leave a note for my ma."

I jot down real quick where I'll be—with her car—and also why there's an open beer on the counter.

"You really don't mind, do you?" she asks as I lock the house up, an unopened can of Coke in her hand.

"Hayles, it's fine." I'm probably more psyched than she is about getting her phone back.

"You are freaking wonderistic, Brody. Why the heck did I not befriend you before now?" She laughs and nudges me with her elbow. My stomach knots up and all the pissed off crap I had from the brief conversation with Gabe just disappears.

She turns, but I grab her hand and whirl her toward me.

Do not *bail out this time, Brody.*

"Hey, uh…" Brain dead. Going brain dead. Just get it out. "W-what are ya doing… I mean…" Ugh. Find the words, dude! "I was wondering if, uh, you had any plans yet for your birthday."

Her eyes widen, and she shakes loose from my hold. "Nothing yet. Why?" Her face is pink. It's so cute like that.

"Can I…" *Do it fast, Brody. Like a band-aid.* "Can I take you out?"

It's out there now. I'm pretty sure it's obvious I'm asking her on a date for real this time. I'm trying to read her expression but it's hard. What is she thinking? At first her mouth pops open, and her eyes light up like I told her she won the lottery—not saying I'm the lottery, but you get what I mean. Next second her green eyes brim over with those tears, and I'm not sure what to think.

So I stand here.

Like an idiot.

Waiting…

Waiting…

Stomach twisting.

Ready to hurl all over the porch.

Still waiting.

How long has it been? Feels like hours.

"A-are you serious?"

Whew. I haven't lost my hearing. "Yeah. I want to take you

out."

"Like on a date?" Her voice pitches on the word.

"Uh, yeah."

Again, I can't read her expression. But it sort-of looks like she thinks I'm making some kind of joke.

"Knock it off, Brody."

Ugh. "I'm serious, Hayles."

Her forehead crinkles, right there between her eyebrows. Does she have any idea how crazy that drives me?

"What? Why?"

Okay, here we go. Can't tell her just *how much* I'm obsessing over her. She'd bolt from the porch, and I'd never see her again. But I can't be too 'whatever' about it either, 'cause she'd never believe me.

I clear my throat. "You deserve to be taken out for your birthday. And... and I want to be the guy who takes you on your first date."

She crosses her arms, making that cleavage pop. I'm going to have to keep my eyes on her face in order to form coherent sentences. "Are you for real?"

"Uh, yeah." Dude, I'm so bad at this. She's going to say no.

Her eyes get watery for the shortest second in the world, but enough for me to worry over it, then... then she's *smiling*. "So, like, what do I wear on a date?" She giggles and hops down the porch. "I've never been on one, remember?"

Just like that, we're back to normalcy. Well, as normal as it ever is between us.

"Something comfortable."

"PJ's?" she jokes.

I laugh and open the door for her, and she plops in. "If you want." Then the images of her in them make me lose concentration for a second.

"Be careful. I'd live in my pajamas if I could."

As I shut the door and cross to my side, I see her feet slide up on the dash, and she taps her knees to a song I'm sure is just in her head. It's like our thing now. Feels like we've been dating for a week already.

Why was I so nervous?

"I take it you're saying yes then?" I ask as I start the engine. I know it's stupid, but I want to hear her say it.

"Yeah... but..."

Oh, here it comes.

"It's not like it's a *real* date or anything. I'm agreeing 'cause you're that awesome of a friend, but we both know sooner or later, you'll be going out with *the* girl. Not just one of your homies."

Grr... this girl!

"It *is* a real date. I want to pick you up and—"

"Can we meet somewhere instead?"

Girl is way weird about her house. Dude, she's weird in general and I'm about to throw in the towel, but I give her a once over, and I can't. She's worth all the trouble.

"I don't want to ruin the surprise." I wink and toss my arm around the back of her headrest. I'm laying it on thick, I know, but she's gotta catch on to the flirting eventually.

"Oh gosh, now I'm nervous!" She laughs and pops open her drink.

"It'll be fun, I promise." I smirk at her before putting the car in drive. "And I'm picking you up. No arguing with me."

She rolls her eyes as she takes a sip of her Coke. "Okay, but like, text me when you're on your way. Deal?"

I can live with that. "Deal." I wrap my hand around hers, and she lets me.

Just like that, we're holding hands. And damn it if I ever let her go.

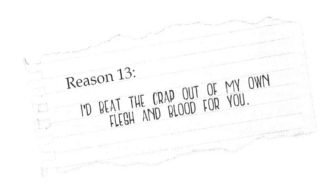

Reason 13:
I'D BEAT THE CRAP OUT OF MY OWN FLESH AND BLOOD FOR YOU.

"Hey ma!" My voice is muffled by all the clothes in my hamper, but Mom hears me.

"What is it?"

I look through the basket again before I yell back up the stairs. "You seen my blue shirt?"

"You have a lot of blue shirts, hun."

Ugh. "You know the long sleeved one with the writing on the arm?"

She doesn't yell back, but I hear her footsteps move to the laundry room and the dryer door swing open.

"It's up here!"

"Will you toss it down?"

I wait to hear the soft thud on the floor outside my room before going out there. Yeah, Mom's not catching me half naked.

Normally I wouldn't care about what kind of shirt I'm wearing, but tonight... yeah, first date with the girl I like and her first date period. Better do my best to look like I care while looking like I don't care.

It's harder than it sounds.

The doorbell rings just as I'm tugging my belt on. If that girl came here instead of letting me pick her up, I'm gonna—

"Quynn!"

Ah hell.

"Hi Terri." Quynn's voice hits me in the stomach. I'm going to crap myself. What is she doing here?

"Come in, come in."

Their footsteps go right to the living room and then the couch creaks as they sit. I take out my cell. Damn it, I'm already running late. Maybe I can crawl out my window.

"Is Brody here?"

In the words of Hayley... how freaking pooptastic! How did I space Quynn was planning on seeing me tonight? Oh that's right, I've been Hayley obsessed. And now I'm stuck. Gotta bail on Quynn... yeah, she said she was coming over to see Mom, and even though it sounds cocky as hell, I know she's here to see me too.

Cell's still in my hand, and I fumble around the keyboard as I try to type Hayles a quick text.

Sry I'm late. I'm coming I promise. Don't u dare start walking over here. I'll text u when I'm close.

Yeah, the last thing I need is for Hayles to show up and see me, Mom, and Quynn talking like it's some sort of messed up book club or something. The image makes my palms sweat.

It's so lame.

"Hey, Quynn's here. Come talk with us."

Yeah, lame isn't a strong enough word.

"I can't." Damn it, I just snapped at my mom. Now she'll know—

"What's wrong?"

I sigh. "Nothing. I'm running late."

"Where are you going?"

"Out."

Tucking my wallet into my back pocket, I try to walk past her, but she blocks me, crossing her arms over her waist in that 'Don't talk to me that way' mother stance.

"Brody, you tell me what's going on right now, or you're not going anywhere."

Ugh. I don't talk girls with Mom. She's biased. She doesn't say it out loud, but I know she wants Quynn and me to…

Yeah, I don't talk girls with Mom.

But I'm honest with my parents.

"I've got a date."

Her arms drop. "Oh."

Yeah, that's all she says.

"Can you tell Quynn I'm sorry, and I'll see her in school?"

Her lips purse together for a second before she says, "You can tell her yourself. You have to walk past her anyway."

She turns to head upstairs, but pauses, hand resting on the handrail. "Is it Hayley?"

I sigh again. Mom's more observant than I thought. And I have been spending a lot of time with Hayles lately. "It's her birthday."

"Oh, okay." Her voice turns upbeat and her smile goes

back on her face. I wish that didn't bug me, but it does. What if it wasn't Hayles' birthday? Why does she care so much about who I decide to date?

Guess I should rephrase. Why does she care so much that I want to date Hayley? I have a guess, but I don't want to even think it, 'cause it'll make me sound like a big dick.

"Tell her I say Happy Birthday."

"I will." I reach over and grab my set of car keys off my dresser. "You okay if I…?"

"Yup, just be careful. And put some gas in it when you're done."

Yeah, I'll have to do that anyway since I'm sure Mom left it on fumes.

I nod, and we both head upstairs, my heart going faster with each step. I don't want to see Quynn's face or smell her citrusy and girly scent. It'll just confuse the crap out of me, and I don't want all that before I'm with Hayles.

Tonight has to be perfect for her, and I won't think about another girl on our first date together. Hayles deserves more than that.

Ugh, am I the right person to do this for her?

"Hey, Brody!"

"Oof!" For a tiny girl, she sure has a lot of force behind her hugs.

Wait... another hug. She's getting a lot more touchy feely with me. Is it all 'cause of those two days I actually used those pointers Hayles gave me?

She pulls back, her face burning red as she tucks the loose strands of hair behind her ear. "Sorry, it feels like I haven't seen you in forever."

I chuckle. It comes out kind of shaky and dorky. "I saw you yesterday."

"Yeah, but we didn't talk. You were... busy."

Awkward. Especially with Mom standing right here.

"Yeah, sorry. Been... preoccupied."

Understatement. I've been obsessed. Following Hayley around trying to figure out what she likes so I can make this

date good for her.

Quynn nods, grabs my hand and pulls me to the couch. I'm a douche, because I whip my hand from hers so hard, I can see it hurt her feelings.

"Sorry, I-I can't stay and talk. Got a..." Why is the word not coming out? *Say it, Brody.* D-A-T-E. *It's not hard.*

"Got plans tonight."

Yup, you're a douche.

"Oh that's right. Friday night is game night." She taps her forehead with the heel of her hand. "Totally forgot."

I should correct her. Mom walked out of the room, and I hear the blender going for whatever frilly drinks she's making for the two of them.

I shouldn't lie.

But I do.

"Yup, so I gotta run." I stand, wiping my sweaty palms on my jeans. "See ya, later?"

She gives me a big smile and nods. "Have fun."

And I bolt out the door before I make more of an ass of myself.

I hate this. This isn't how tonight was supposed to start. I've got a date with the most freaking awesome girl, and then Quynn shows up, messing with my head. Why is it so hard to tell her I'm with someone else?

Well, I'm not really with Hayley... but I want to be.

I kick the potted plant that has long ago died, knocking all the dirt and dead leaves on the lawn.

"What's up your ass?"

It's as if God knew I needed a punching bag. Either that, or He thinks He's real funny. Gabe takes a puff of his... nope that ain't a cigarette, as he leans against Mom's car.

"What are you doing here?"

He shrugs and takes another drag, coughing before he talks. "Waiting for Mark to get home."

Oh, so he's waiting to get the snot beat out of him. Not that Dad would do that, but Dad's the only person who hasn't said one word to Gabe since the whole cheating on his girl, moving out, and quitting his job thing.

And smoking pot isn't going to help anything. He's such an idiot.

"Well, move. I gotta go."

He doesn't.

"You're leaving?" He pauses to puff. "Thought you'd stay to get some action with my ex."

My teeth snap shut, and I'm holding in all the crazy stuff going on in my chest. "It's not like that," I growl. "I'm not like you and Dad, who'll just bang anybody with more money than who they're with."

I know I hit a sore spot, but I don't give a damn. Bringing up biological Daddy might knock some sense into my brother's empty head.

But he just throws me a smirk.

"You know, you think I'm the bad guy, but if you just get your head out of your ass for a second, you'd get it. Why I did what I did."

Whose head is in whose ass?

"Move."

He shrugs again and steps away from the car. We don't say a word as I get in and start the engine. Good. I don't want any conversation with my douchebag brother to ruin this night with Hayles.

I'm ready to pull out, but Gabe sticks his face in the window. The weed smell is going to make me blow chunks all over his stupid grin.

"Have fun with the wide load."

Hell no.

I'm not even thinking. Don't care that I'm not thinking. The door swings open with so much force it knocks Gabe flat on his butt. Don't know how I get there, but I'm on top of him, punching his damn nose into his damn skull.

There's a sick satisfaction to beating the shit out of my brother. Knowing I can is good, but everything bothering me gets unleashed on him. Blow after blow, they sabotage my head and explode onto Gabe's dumbass face. The stupid obsession I have over Quynn, the way I feel about Hayles and no one understanding why, including Hayley herself, what he did to our family, and just how stupid he is and how stupid I am for acting just like him. Dragging around two girls because I can't make up my mind.

It's then as I put another knuckle in his mouth that I catch a glimpse of the tatt I've got on my wrist. The one I got right after Gabe ran out. And even though I was supposed to help put Quynn back together, I *wanted* to put her back together, I was the one who fell apart. And she picked me up, dusted me off, and I…

Fell for another girl.

My arm stops mid-punch, and I stare into Gabe's face which is now so bloody and swollen, I can barely tell he's still smirking underneath it all.

"Brody?" Mom's voice feels like a thousand jagged knives in my back. "G-Gabe?"

I know I shouldn't look, but I do. My eyes flick to her and

Quynn, standing on the porch, both with the same expression on their faces.

I gotta get out of here.

Shaking, I shove off my brother and dive in the car. The tires squeal as I full throttle it down the road.

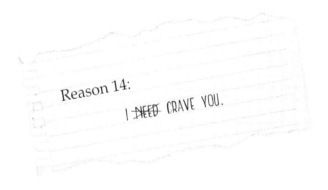

Reason 14:
I ~~NEED~~ CRAVE YOU.

I'm late. Really late. First date for Hayles, and I'm beyond any excuse. But I have to sort out my head before I see her. Because I know once I'm with her, there will be little thought process.

I'm pulled over about a block away from her house, half expecting her to come skipping—no, she'd be stomping by this point—down the sidewalk and finding me here.

Is it wrong for me to like Hayley? To want her and not Quynn. Am I just as bad as Gabe and the dad I don't normally claim? I stare at my tattoo again and trace the symbol, but that only reminds me of when Hayles did that in class a few days ago.

I wonder what she'd think about this. Say I was falling for a different girl other than Hayles. Would she slap me and tell me to stay focused on Quynn, or would she tell me to go after the new girl?

Oh dude. I'm so dumb. Making a big deal over this. I have no claim on Quynn. I *never* did. And she has no claim on me. I'm feeling guilty over something I haven't done, but why? I'm figuring out what I want *before* making a mess like my brother did.

And I want Hayley.

How could I want anyone else? She's amazing, that girl. Damn sexy, funny, and just knows how to make me feel... all that crap you're supposed to feel when you're with the girl you just have to be around.

I need her.

No, I *crave* her.

And right now, I'm being a real jackhole 'cause I'm over an hour late for her first date, not only with me, but ever.

Okay, Brody. Erase all that crap about Quynn, about Gabe, and just be with Hayles tonight. It's her night.

It's like I'm on autopilot, and I'm at her house without knowing how I got there. She's sitting on her porch steps, picking the leaves off the bush next to her. Her hair is down. I've never seen it that way before. It's so long, coming just under her boobs, which are definitely amazing in the shirt she's wearing. Low cut, but not so low that I can see anything more than just a little cleavage. Damn sexy.

Then I remember. Shit. I was supposed to text her before I picked her up. This is not going my way.

I jog up the walk, and she doesn't look at me. Still picking at that bush.

"Are you mad?"

That's the dumbest question in the history of questions. I'm really making this a memorable date for her.

Her eyes flick to my face, and what looked like anger flashes to confusion. Forehead puckers in that cute way of hers, and her mouth pops open. "I *was* a little peeved." She stands. "But now I'm more worried about that look on your face. Are you okay?"

No. Quynn's at my house, and I just beat my brother's face in. And I spent who knows how long in the car trying to calm down. But right now I'm with Hayles, and I don't want to think about all that crap.

"I'm fine."

I scratch my nose, what I always do when I lie my face off... which is why I don't lie to my parents 'cause they know this.

"Gracious little fairies, Brody!" She grabs my hand. "You're bleeding!"

Yeah, bloody and swollen knuckles. My hands are shaking too. Don't know how I missed it. It's pouring rivers down the back of my wrist.

"Would you look at that." *Smooth, Brody. On top of being a jackass, you're now an idiot.*

She tugs me inside, not letting go of my arm and nearly sprinting to her kitchen sink. Can't even process that I'm in her house. Only thing going through my brain is her touching my skin, running water over my knuckles and washing my arm. The blood doesn't bug her or nothing. Her face isn't calm, worried as hell, but I like that.

She's worried about me.

I know I'm testing my boundaries, and I have no right to be this close to her after showing up late with bloody knuckles, but I trap her between me and the sink, leaning over her head. She still has that mint chocolately scent, but it's mixed with some sort of fruity lotion or something. Things are moving down south just off her smell.

Yeah. Hayles is definitely the girl I want. I can't even remember why I was so confused before.

I almost whip her around and kiss her, but she lets go of my hand and ducks under my arm, going for the freezer.

"I don't need that," I say as she pulls out the ice pack. "I'll be fine."

"You sure?" She tosses it between her hands, face going a little pink.

I shut off the water. "Yeah. It feels better already." 'Cause it does.

She grabs a towel from the counter. "Heads up." She tosses it over her shoulder as she puts the ice pack back in the freezer.

I wonder if she even realizes I'm in her house. The one place she doesn't let anyone near. It's not a craphole, which is what I expected since she treats it like the plague. It's clean, and there's a buttload of expensive stuff. Stainless steel appliances and place settings at the table even though it doesn't look like anyone's going to be eating soon. There's framed flowers and other crap like that hanging on the walls. Looks like I've walked into one of those showcase houses.

But she's giving me one of those 'are you really okay?' smiles, so pretty sure my hand is all she's concerned about right now.

Again... I like that.

I'm losing control over my body. Don't know how I end up where I do—inches away from her—but she doesn't shy away. She grabs my hand from under the towel and pokes the skin around the cuts.

"You going to tell me what happened? Or will I have to guess?"

I smile. "You like guessing games."

She shakes her head and tries not to smile back, but fails. "All right. I'll try to guess on our way to... wherever it is we're going." She pauses. "I mean, if we're still going out."

"He... heck yeah. It's your birthday." Crap. That should've been the first thing I said to her. "Uh... Happy Birthday." *It's a little late now, Brody.*

Her smile fills her face. "Thanks." Then she tugs me outside like the place is going to blow.

"Okay, be honest," she says just as we get to the car. "Is what I'm wearing date appropriate? I tried to go comfortable like you said, but still... girls dress up for stuff like this, right?"

She's giving me permission to check her out, which I've been doing since she walked me to the gas station in the rain, but now I don't have to be discreet or anything. Sweet.

And yeah, she looks sexy as hell. Now that I'm closer, I can see how soft her hair looks draped over her rack, and she's got on one of those big belt girls wear around their stomachs and it hugs her curved body making her look thinner than she is.

"Brody?"

"Yeah, sorry." I open the car door and try to get the calm cool guy to come out, instead of this nervous pervert who keeps looking at her cleavage. "You look hot, Hayles. And it's definitely appropriate for what we're going to be doing."

Something in my stomach goes *wa-bam!* She's going to love what I got planned for her tonight.

She plops in the seat and puts her feet on the dash. I'm smiling like a fool, but everything… I mean all of that stuff I was dealing with before I headed over here, it's just… gone.

"Okay, home fry," she says as I get in the car, "where are we going?" Her voice is calm and all gangster-like, but by the look of her face and the sexy spark in her green eyes, she's excited.

And I get excited off her getting excited.

"Surprise."

"No, no, no." Her lip juts out. "Please tell me."

It's hard not to give into that look, but at the same time, I like the effect I'm having on her.

"Nope."

Instead of begging and whining like most girls would, her mouth turns up into the hugest of evil grins, and she turns the station on the radio, lands on Katy Perry, then cranks it up to burst your eardrums level.

She's good.

But I'm not caving.

And I shock the crap out of her by bursting out in song with her. By the end of the song we're both laughing our faces off, and that's the first time in the history of ever I've liked listening to pop.

"Okay," she says as she turns the music down and wipes her eyes, "well played, Mr. Grant. Well played."

I laugh and try to be smooth about grabbing her hand. Pretend to go for the radio, but she sees right through it and yanks her hand away like I'm about to taze her.

Damn it.

"Uh…" She looks out the window. "Are we going downtown?"

"That okay?"

Her smile swallows her face when she looks back at me. "Oh, heck yes!"

She's too cute. Can't believe I'm on a date with her. And I don't care she's not wanting to, I offer my hand, sticking it out in an obvious, 'hold my hand or I may die' kind of way. She looks at it, looks at me, then giggles and tucks her fingers between mine.

No suave Faberge—or whatever that butter commercial guy's

name is—but hey, it works.

We talk, and she tries to get me to tell her about my hand, but I won't. I don't want to ruin this night by talking about Gabe. And I also don't have the brain power either since I'm focusing on trying not to sweat a waterfall into her palm. Trip takes about twenty minutes—doesn't seem that long—then I'm pulling in the parking lot.

"Mother of a pearl necklace."

Just the reaction I wanted. I grin, let go of her hand—I'll get it back in a second—and get out of the car to open the door for her.

"This okay?"

"Are you for real?" she asks as she steps out.

"Only if you still want to."

She eyes the sign out front, the bright neon flashing INFINITY TATTOO. When she turns to me, she leaps into my arms so fast I lose balance and crash into the hood of the car.

"Whoops! Sorry." Her face goes bright red as she climbs off me, but I pull her back, keeping her hand strapped to my swollen one.

"I take that as a 'yes'?"

She nods, dragging me inside.

"I know *exactly* what I want to get!"

Darn girl can't stand still. She's bouncing around with a huge smile, and even though she just said she knows what she wants, she's looking at all the options.

And I can't keep my hands off her. But she's letting me, so I lean over her like I did in her kitchen, breathing in her scent as she flips through the laminated pages.

There's a flush in the back and a few seconds later, London comes walking out from the crapper, drying his hands off on some paper towels before chucking them in the garbage.

"Hey, Brody," he says as he makes his way behind the counter and we clasp hands and bump shoulders. I accidentally smack Hayles in the back of the head with my chin and she ducks out from underneath me. I was pushing my limits anyway.

"How's it going?"

"Same shit."

I take a glance at Hayles' face, but I must've missed the cringe, or she's too distracted to notice London's cursing.

"So, you here to get some more ink?"

"Actually—"

"I'm getting one!" Hayley's still bouncing as she looks at London, big smile on her face. "It's my first one! Yay!"

London barks out laughing, and I want to sock him if he's making fun of her, but he leans forward, looking at the book she's got and says, "Do you have anything in mind?"

She flips through more pages, and her lips turn into an incredibly sexy pout. "I can't find it."

London waves his hand in the air, leaning closer to her.

Wait a second. Is he hitting on her?

"I really want something that'll represent like, passion or love or something. Nothing too girly and frilly and stuff, but something that's like, sexy."

"Hmm…" He moves from the counter, and I take a step closer to Hayles. I know it's possessive, but I don't care. She's my date.

"How about the lotus?" He grabs a couple pieces of art work from the back counter and sets them in front of her. "It's a flower, which is girly, I know, but… if you want, I can make it smoky. You see this one here?"

He points to the one in the top right of the page, red smoke curling around a dark purple, near black lotus flower. It looks like it was the only thing remaining from a fire. It's pretty badass for a chick tatt.

"Oh my gosh, yes! That's the one I want. It's freaking beautiful!"

"Thanks. I designed this last week. Haven't been able to use it yet."

Hayles starts to bounce up and down again and I slide my arm around her waist. She recoils, and I drop my arm and go for a 'I was just trying to put my hand in my back pocket the long way' kind of thing. I look like an idiot.

And London's eyes are locked on her boobs. Because I have a complex or something, I blurt out, "Hey, I was hoping to add on to mine while we're here."

That's a big lie. But no way is he getting his hands on her. I'll make him work on me instead.

"Really? You're going to do it with me?" Hayley's eyes brighten and dude, she looks so happy, I'm glad I came up with the BS even if it means I gotta get stabbed in the wrist again.

"Yeah."

"Sa-weet!" She grabs my wrist and yanks off the leather band I keep around it. "What are you going to do?"

"Yeah, Bro..." London smiles, leaning against the counter again... towards Hayles. "What kind of add on are you looking to get?"

Maybe it's 'cause I'm a douche, but I feel like punching him in the mouth. But my already sore knuckles tell me it's not worth it. The flirting may be my imagination anyways.

"I dunno. Like a chain or something to wrap the two symbols together?"

"Oh! That'll look supa awesome." Hayles traces around the ink on my wrist, making swirly patterns between the marks already there. "That reminds me..." She drops my hand. "You never told me what they mean."

London cocks an eyebrow as he tongues his lip ring. He pushes off the counter and goes into the back, leaving us alone.

"Later?"

She huffs, but smiles. "Okay, but you owe me that story."

"I know, I know."

We're quiet while she flips through more designs... well, I'm quiet. She's humming a song under her breath and tapping her foot.

"You know..." Voice-box shuts down. I was going to tell her how amazing her voice is, but I've lost my nerve. And I can't think of anything else to say.

"Was there an end to that sentence?" She giggles, shuts the book and leans on it.

Yes. "I guess not."

She laughs again.

"All right!"

London comes out with Marisa, the other artist in the shop. She's got next to nothing on top, and her gauged ears have pen caps in them. She gives us both a wide smile and says, "Okay, I call that hot piece of ass."

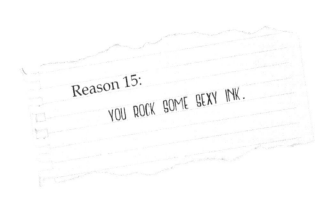

Reason 15:
YOU ROCK SOME SEXY INK.

I must be really arrogant, 'cause I swear Marisa was referring to my 'hot piece of ass', but she links elbows with Hayles and brings her into the back room, London protesting the whole way.

"No you don't. I designed the lotus she wants. I get to put it on her."

And Hayley thinks she's not hot? She better after this display of two older tattoo artists fighting over who gets to put ink on her. Man, I wish I had the talent to do it, so I could get a vote thrown my way.

"Yo, London." Better make it easy for them. "I'd like you to do the chain on mine if you don't mind." *Think of a good reason, Brody.* "You know, since you did this one." I point to my wrist like a damn fool.

"Fine." He looks at Marisa who's sticking her tongue out. "But I get to do the next lotus."

"Deal."

Hayley's face is bright red, looking a little awkward. She catches my eye, throws me a grin and inches toward my hand. I grasp hers before she has a chance to change her mind.

"Okay, first thing's first." Marisa squirts a glob of hand sanitizer in her palm and rubs it around. "You got ID?"

Hayles nods, pulling her license from her back pocket. Marisa takes a quick look, then a double take, then squeals. "Nice. Birthday tatt?"

"Yep. Isn't Brody an awesome buddy?"

Does she still not get that this is. A. Date? How can I be more obvious?

"Sure is." Marisa hands back the ID, then gives us all the paperwork we gotta fill out. After twenty minutes of answering all the questions, Marisa says, "Now, tell me where you want it."

"Hmm…" Hayles pats her body, talking under her breath. I don't know if I'm meant to hear it, but I do.

Her fingers prod her hip bone. "No… too chubby for that one." Darn girl. She moves to her butt. "Maybe, but not sure if I want a flower next to the hole I use for waste, though it would make sense to put one there."

I have to force back the laughter barreling from my mouth. Gotta turn it into one of those lame coughs. Hayles is still talking to herself as she runs her hands over her body. The boobs are out because 'they're not done growing'. If that's true, I'm in trouble. The stomach and sides are also a no because of the 'chubby' thing. Girl is crazy. And the feet and ankles were a 'fricking NOT happening' because that would hurt more than a 'bunch of lobsters in a hot tub'.

She looks up at Marisa, a slight frown on her face and her eyebrows creased right there in the middle that drives me insane.

"How about here?" I know it's an excuse to touch her, but I don't care. I gently press her left shoulder blade. Goose bumps crawl up her neck, and she shivers. Blush fills her checks as she looks at me with a big smile.

"Yep. That's where I want it." She shrugs off my hand. Okay, point taken. She's still not into the touching. "Thanks, Brody."

I nod and tuck my hands in my pockets to keep from moving them all over her. Won't push my luck anymore tonight.

"'Kay, come have a seat right here…" Marisa pats the chair in the right corner. "And Brody you can have the station next to her if you want to watch."

REASONS I FELL FOR THE FUNNY FAT FRIEND

"Yeah, please sit next to me," says as she takes her place in the seat Marisa pointed to. "I need someone to blabber to, 'cause I'm a little nervous."

For a second I get real stupid and think she's talking about being nervous about me. That I make her nervous. But duh... not me, the needle that'll be stabbing her makes her more nervous than I ever will.

And I should not be jealous of a tatt gun.

I plop down at the station next to Hayles, waiting for London to bring me a design to look over. Marisa says she'll be right back, and then it's silent.

I should say something, but nothing is going through my brain. Hayley *does* look nervous, which is cute because I've never really seen her like this.

"You all right there, jumpy?"

She purses her lips together and nods like her head is going to fall off if she moves it too much.

"Liar."

She throws me a sort of smile then starts tapping her knees.

"It's not so bad. Yours is small. It'll take maybe forty-five minutes. Hour tops."

"Yeah."

Silence.

"Hayles?"

"Huh?"

"You don't have to do this if you don't want to. I just thought... you said you really wanted to, and I should've... you know, maybe should've asked you before—"

"Knock it off, Brody. I totally want to do this! Weren't you a little nervous your first time?"

I shrug. Not really. I was more pissed off, and the pain didn't outweigh the other crap I was dealing with.

"That and I guess..." She shakes her head. "Nevermind."

"What?"

"Nothing, I forget."

110

Liar.

"Hayles…"

She pretends to zip her lips, but then her mouth splits open into a real smile.

"Fine. But I'll get it outta ya sooner or later."

Cocking her head to the side, she moves her gaze to the floor. "Hey, Brody? Where are you from?"

"What?"

"Your accent. I've always been curious about it."

I smirk. "I lived in Oklahoma for a while. Probably where I got it from."

"That's way awesome! Any of your other family have accents too?"

"Just my brother. Mom's from here."

"Oh, so what about your dad?"

I forget sometimes she's only known me for a little while. That she doesn't know that mentioning bio-dad sets my body on fire. But with her, I don't mind talking about it.

"Yeah, that's where my mom and dad met. When they got divorced, we moved to Oregon."

"Wait, so do you have a step-dad? Or is it just you and your mom?"

"Step-dad. They've been married for a while now."

She starts twisting her fingers, cracking them. Don't know if it's 'cause of the conversation or 'cause of the tattoo still, but she's way nervous.

"You like him?"

I give her a big smile when she looks at me. "He's cool. More of a dad than my real dad was."

"That's awesome." She stops cracking her knuckles. "What's it like in Oklahoma? I haven't been anywhere. Lived in the same house my whole life and only been to the major cities around here, but not often. Like, this tattoo shop is a vacation for me."

"Oh, should I bring in some Slippery Nipples?" Marisa laughs at her own joke, Hayles cracking up with her, but I think it's more of the nerves coming into play.

"You know alcohol isn't good for tatts," London says as he straps on his gloves and takes a seat next to me. He shows me a couple of designs, and I probably should be paying more attention to him, but I'm watching Hayles try to sit still while Marisa talks her through everything. Then she has her pull her shirt off her shoulder, and I've lost all train of thought.

London snaps in front of my face.

"Yo!"

Whoops.

"You okay with this one?" He's smirking at me.

I think I say yes, but I don't really get a good look. I trust London, even though he's been checking out Hayles' tits this entire time.

He presses the stencil on my wrist, tugs off slowly, and yeah, it's cool looking, so I don't tell him nevermind or anything.

I hear Marisa's gun go on, and she leans over Hayley's back. "Try to relax, okay, hot stuff?"

Hayley nods, takes a glance at me, throwing out a scared smile. Two seconds later, the needle pierces the skin on her shoulder.

Her mouth pops open, but no sound comes out. She shuts her eyes real tight and starts mouthing something, but I can't figure out what she's saying.

We're all quiet, except for the buzzing from the tatt guns. My wrist burns, but I'm distracted enough to not really notice. I can't keep my eyes off Hayley's face, her skin, the way she's keeping it together even though I know it hurts like hell.

"Brody?" Her eyes open. "Distract me please?"

I chuckle, trying to keep my wrist still. "You want me to sing more Katy Perry?"

Her laughter bursts from her strained mouth, like she'd been holding her breath this whole time.

"Okay, tell me another one."

"What?"

"Tell me another joke."

I get an evil look from Marisa who's trying to keep Hayley still through all the giggles. Too bad. Hayles could ask me anything and I'd do it. She's got me.

"Should I rhyme words with 'fart'?"

She laughs again, relaxing under the needle. "I think we covered all those words."

"Did you mention 'shart'?" Marisa asks, stifling her own laughter and taking the gun away from Hayley's skin.

Both Hayles and I go into hysterics. London and Marisa have to wait for us to calm down enough to keep still.

"Didn't realize we were inking twelve-year-olds," Marisa says with a grin. Hayley throws me a look that gets my stomach twisted. Yeah, I like having inside jokes with her too.

Both our tatts only take about thirty-five minutes. I pay for both—because this is a date!—and ignore all of Hayley's protests and reassurance that she'll 'totally pay me back'.

I wait till we're in the car to ask, "Can I see it?"

Her shirt's still hanging off her shoulder, but she's twisted in a way that I can't make out her new ink. At first I think she's going to say no, but then she brushes her hair off her neck and turns, so I can get a good look.

I can feel the heat coming from her, but I'm not sure if it's 'cause I'm making her nervous or if it's 'cause she's just been stabbed a million times. The tatt is pretty hot. All right, really hot. So hot I have to adjust myself. Never thought I'd be into a girl who had ink, but looking at the smoke lines from the flower going across her shoulder blade and almost touching her neck, dude, I want to run my fingers over it.

I don't. I learned my lesson.

"Is it that bad?"

I gulp. "No, i-it's… nice."

Ugh. Lamest compliment ever.

She cranes her neck, resting her chin on her shoulder, her eyes flicking up to meet mine. "I guess that's good."

"Uh huh."

Just like that, I'm leaning in to kiss her.

And she leans back, face going as red as mine probably is. "Um, what are you doing?"

Okay, okay, I should give her the benefit of the doubt here. She's never been kissed, so maybe she doesn't know what it looks like.

No, that's stupid. Of course she knows what I was doing. And she doesn't want me to.

Crap.

"Sorry, you uh, have an eyelash." And I had to get it off with my lips.

"Oh!" A huge breath escapes her mouth, punching me in the face. I'm a cocky butt, 'cause I expected shock, hesitation, maybe a 'I'm not ready yet for that', but not... *relief.*

Because I can't deal with another rejection, I snap on my seatbelt and start the car, then do a burnout from the parking lot.

Hayley's quiet, not singing or playing with the radio. I don't know how that makes me feel 'cause maybe the tension in the air will finally make her *get it.* But, still, I feel like a jerk for throwing a fit over it and making her uncomfortable on her birthday. And her first date.

Crap.

"Hey, so you hungry?" I smile, a really big and probably creepy looking smile.

She breaks the tension, another huge breath going out her mouth. "Starving." Then she hits the radio and puts her feet on the dash.

Even though I kind of want to, I can't stay mad at her. She's never led me on or anything. Been pretty clear about where I stand with her.

I'm just pissed at myself I guess.

Reason 16:
YOU MAKE ME FEEL ALL THAT GOOEY
~~SHIT~~ STUFF I'M SUPPOSED TO FEEL.

Despite that awkward moment in the car, I'm able to just chill with Hayles the rest of the night. After tossing straw wrappers at each other, she dumped the entire salt shaker in my drink. I'm not talking about taking the lid off and pouring salt in it, but grabbing the salt shaker and plopping it in the glass. Waitress wasn't too happy, but I was rolling.

After the restaurant—and Hayles stabbing me with her fork when I went after her croutons—she drug me into a grocery store and we picked pretend fights when people walked down the aisle we were in. She bought me a Coke to make up for the one she 'salted', and we drove around for about an hour doing nothing but talking about the different ways to say 'Hell'.

"Sometimes I say, 'what the h?' just like 'WTF'. People don't always get it though." She shrugs.

"And they get 'holy horse feathers'?" I chuckle as she punches me in the arm.

Pulling into her driveway, I snap off the headlights even though she didn't ask me to this time. I wish I wasn't out of money and gas. I'd keep her out all night.

She clicks the seatbelt, and I bolt around the car to beat her to the door. She laughs as she steps out.

"Thanks, Brody."

"Uh huh."

I close the door and walk her up the porch. Part of me wonders if she'll notice I'm taking her to the front door, which she's never allowed before, but she turns around and leaps into my arms so fast again, I'm almost knocked on my back.

"I mean it. Thank you," she says against my cheek. "I told you I haven't had the best track record with birthdays, and well, this was the best one I've had."

What is this girl doing to me? I squeeze her back, wishing I could keep her locked in my arms forever, but I won't. The second she gets uncomfortable, I'll let go.

She loosens her grip, but doesn't jump away from me. That gives the bruised ego an icepack. Her fingers linger on the tatt on my wrist, and it itches like crap. Not going to tell her to stop though.

"Hey, Hayles?"

Her eyes flick up to mine. "Sup?"

I smile. "Can I... I mean, can we go out again?"

"Like as friends?"

No.

I gulp. "Another date. I want to..." Grr, why is this so hard? "I want to be with you, Hayley."

I can't read her expression. She takes a step back, not touching me. I've never seen her bite her lip, so when it tucks between her teeth I have no idea what it means.

"Why?"

"Why what?"

"Why do you want to be with *me*? Is this some kind of pity thing? Because I'm not interested."

Is she for real? "Hayles, you're killing me!" I'm not sure what it is. The left over anger from dealing with Gabe, or the nerves I've had all night just trying to get the words out, but suddenly I'm saying things I'd never—and boy do I mean never—thought I'd say.

"I've been trying all night with you. It's hard enough putting myself out there, but even harder when I gotta explain myself, but if you need to hear why, then I'll tell you." I take a deep breath and grab her hand. I'm not going to let her shake me off this time. "I like you, all right? I want to date you not out of pity, but because I... I *need* to. Hayles, I can't get you off my mind."

There it is.

Just like that, I've vomited all my gushy feelings all over her.

And she's just staring at me.

Staring and sort-of smiling.

I don't want one of her sort-of smiles. I want a real Hayles smile. The one that makes her eyes crinkle in the corners.

"W-what about Quynn?" she finally says, her voice just above a whisper.

"I told you. I'm not... she's not... I don't feel that way about her anymore."

Her eyes drop to our hands, and she blows out a huge breath. "Holy jumping jellybeans, Brody. When did this happen?"

I chuckle, and it relieves some of the tension in my chest. "What do you mean?"

"I'm trying to rewind here. Find out what exactly was the turning point. What did I do to make you feel like this?"

Ah hell, so many things. Too many things to list. I like everything about this girl. How can she not see how freaking awesome she is?

"You've got one heck of a personality, Hayles. Plus..." *Say it Brody. You're on a roll.* "You're gorgeous."

My face is red, I'm sure of it, but it can't be anywhere near the shade of hers.

I've so got this. Don't know why I was so nervous, or why I thought it would be harder than this to convince her. I mean, she looks so...

Wait a minute.

Her eyes are getting watery.

What did I say?

"Hey, what's wrong?" I ask as I take a step closer to her.

Tears pour down her cheeks as she shakes her head toward the ground.

There's no way I'm just going to stand here and let her cry. I take her in my arms and hold her. The tension is back in my chest, but it feels good that she's allowing me to touch her like this. She sobs into my shirt, but doesn't wrap her arms around me. I'm okay with that, even though I have no idea what's going on.

"Hayles, did I say something wrong?" I ask over her head.

She shakes her head, and her voice muffles in my shirt. "Brody, I-I can't believe you."

"What do you mean?"

She pushes away from me and sucks in a large breath. "I *can't* believe everything you're saying to me. I-I'm not going to."

Not sure how to react. Part of me wants to drop it all, forget getting Hayles and go back to Quynn. That's a prick of a thing to say, still, can't help but feel it'd be easier.

Thinking about it though, I couldn't do that. At all. The whole time I'd be with Quynn—hypothetically, of course, since that won't happen either—I'd want to be with Hayley. And that's a Gabe thing, not a Brody thing.

I'm a fighter too. And I'll keep fighting until she gets a restraining order.

"Why not?" Rejection sucks. I should at least know why she keeps pushing me off. "I get it if you're not into me. Just say the 'friend' word, and I won't bring it up again."

"That's not it." She sniffs and brushes her hair off her shoulder. "It's just… what happens when Quynn finally comes around?"

"Huh?"

"Brody…" She plops on the porch, and I take a seat next to her. "Did you forget what I told you about Jason? About why I set the rules upfront?"

"I remember."

"Then why are you doing this to me? Are you really that mean?"

What the hell?

"What are you talking about?"

"I'm not going to be the girl you use while you wait for *the* girl to give you the time of day. I thought you were better than that."

She thinks I'm using her? I repeat. What. The. Hell?

"I'm not like that."

She rolls her eyes. "You're saying you actually want to be with *me*, when you could have someone like *her*? Yeah, okay."

I'm starting to get pissed. This girl doesn't get it. Doesn't get how amazing she is. How much I've been panting over her since we started hanging out. How many times I chose her over Quynn already.

"I told you, I don't want Quynn. I want you."

She cocks an eyebrow, folding her arms and leaning on her knees. "And how many times did you think about her tonight?"

I do a mental checklist 'cause I want to be honest. Thought about her before I got to Hayley's house, but I was also thinking about Hayles. Other than that...

"I didn't."

She opens her mouth to argue, but I cut her off.

"I *didn't*, Hayles. You were the only thing on my mind."

She falls on her knees, her hair covering her face and exposing her new ink. Her back goes up and down with each deep breath she takes. Wish I knew what she was thinking. Maybe this is just an excuse 'cause she doesn't look at me the way I want her to.

I'm a fool. All this time she was dodging my touch and avoiding the compliments was because she didn't want to lead me on. Not 'cause of her insecurities. But 'cause she doesn't want me the same way I want her.

Now I feel like shit. Should've just taken the first rejection and left it alone.

"I-I get it if you don't want to... I mean if I'm not your type or anything." Crap, gotta wipe the sweat off my palms. It's starting to sting the cuts on my knuckles. "Just thought you needed to know how I felt about you."

"Gosh, Brody. That's. Not. It." Her head tilts up. "I've been trying... I mean *really* trying not to get all gushy ga-ga over you. It's not the easiest thing in the world. I had to keep pushing myself away from you, keep telling myself that all the stuff you were doing was because you were my friend. All the hand holding and smiling and looking hecka hot was because that's just who you are. You want Quynn. That's what I keep telling myself."

She takes a breath, finally looking me in the eyes. "You deserve someone like her anyway. Someone who's… beautiful."

"You are b—"

"You know what I mean." Her hands cover her stomach. A tear strolls down her cheek. "I'm fat, all right. Don't argue with me because I'm not stupid. I see the way people look at me, and I hear what they say. You and I… we just won't make sense. People won't understand it." She pauses. "*I* don't understand it."

Okay, so she doesn't want me to argue, but no way am I agreeing with her on the fat thing. I take her hands in mine, playing with her fingers. She's shaking, I'm shaking, and the weird thing is, I'm not nervous. Not now. Not after she told me exactly what's stopping her. This, I can deal with, because she's wrong.

"All right, so even if you were fat, which you're *not*, why would it matter? Why can't we be together if we feel the same things for each other?"

She shakes her head, more tears dropping from her eyelashes as she blinks. "It doesn't make sense. Why would anyone choose the fat girl over the skinny one?" She grips my hand and stares me down. "You tell me that, and maybe… maybe I can allow myself to feel the things I want to feel for you."

"You want reasons why you and not Quynn?" I don't want her to think I'm saying she's fat, so I add, "Why I want a gorgeous and crazy funny girl I just met instead of the one I've been looking at for a while?"

Her cheeks flush, and she scoots closer. "Yes. That's exactly what I want."

Great! I have this in the bag. I can list a million things right now.

"Okay, reason one—"

"No. I want you to write them down for me. Give me time to

process all this, and you to make sure they're good." She smiles. A real Hayley smile.

"Yes, ma'am!" I salute, and she punches me in the arm. Just like that, we're back in the 'friend' arena. Friend arena with potential.

She stands and helps me up. I keep my hand tucked in hers, and wish I could go in for the kiss. Not going to do that again. Not when I'm this close to getting her.

"Happy Birthday, Hayles."

Smiling, she pulls me into a hug. "Thank you again, Mr. Grant. Best freaking night of my gosh darn life. Even with you bearing your soul and all."

I chuckle as she lets me go. I watch her walk into the house and stand out there till my feet feel like moving again.

Bam! Best date ever, even with all that awkward crap it wasn't... awkward. Better put that on the list.

She's got the best smile, knows how to have fun, and makes me feel gooey and stuff. Putting those on there too.

This list will be the easiest thing in the world.

Reason 17:

YOU'RE A CUTE LITTLE CHEATER.

This crap is hard.

I can come up with all the reasons I need to, but when I write them down they look so stupid.

That and my hand is so sore my handwriting looks like I just learned how to write ten seconds before I started this list.

I stare at the paper with scribble marks all over it and chuck it in the corner of the ass room. Yes, it's become the corn chippy room again because all I did after dropping Hayles off is text the crap out of her and lay in bed, thinking about that tatt on her shoulder. I bet it's healed enough now I can touch it. Run my fingers over it and press my lips against it.

You know… if she ever lets me.

I can't concentrate on this right now. I have to get in that cheesy goobery mood, and I'm just not feeling it. I don't want to write it all down because I want to talk to her. Plopping down on the bed, I whip out my phone and press the only contact I ever call in there.

After four rings I know she's not picking up. I leave a lame message, the 'hey it's me… uh, Brody, yeah… call me back' one that makes me sound way more awkward than I'd like.

Because I'm bored—and just a bit obsessive—I grab my jacket and head out. Sunday afternoon and I got nothing better to do than drive past Hayley's house. 'Cause I just have to.

"Where you going?" Dad puts his glasses back on as he sits up on the couch, blinking his eyes as he tries to get the sleep out of them from his old man nap.

"Just out for a bit." I grab the keys. "You okay if I take your car?" Dad's truck is much cooler than Mom's Corsica, but also Hayley won't recognize it.

"Tell you what, you sit here and talk to the old man for two minutes, and you can take the Dodge."

Sounds like a good deal to me. Except this is probably about the face surgery I gave Gabe on Friday. I sit down on the edge of the seat. I know Dad won't beat me or anything, but still… defense mode is molded into my body.

"You want to tell me what happened with Gabe? Or should I just go with what he told me?"

I set my elbows on my knees. "He's an ass."

"If that's the only reason you beat his mug, then it would've happened before now."

This is why Dad's cool. Why I didn't completely crap myself when he asked me and Gabe if he could marry Mom. Why I call him Dad and not Mark. Because he gets it. He just knows everything that goes down and doesn't freak, but talks about it. Dude, Gabe was here to see *him*, because even though Dad hasn't talked to him since he bailed on our family, he knew he would listen.

I run my hand over my buzzed head. "He said something that threw me over the edge. I don't know what happened, but I couldn't stop."

"From what your Mom said, you did stop."

I shrug. They're right. I did stop once I saw what an idiot I was being. And how stupid it was for me to take out all the stuff I was dealing with on him. Even though the punk deserved it. Still, I punched him long and hard enough he needed stitches. I feel maybe ten percent bad about it.

"What did he say?"

No. Not going to tell him about Hayles. It sucks already that she thinks she's the 'FFF' or whatever she called it, but having Gabe say it, then telling Dad about it… no. It's not happening.

I don't care what she or anyone else thinks. She's not fat.

"Nothing. Just pissed me off."

Dad leans forward, looking at me over his glasses. "It was about a girl, wasn't it?"

How in the hell?

"Huh?"

"Come on, son. I get it. Whenever someone says something about your mother, or cops a feel or something, I want to do the same thing to them. It's built in our DNA. We protect the girls we love."

I'm trying real hard to ignore he just said people 'cop a feel' on my mom. Ugh.

"Yeah."

He chuckles. "I won't pry, but I should probably get some discipline in here somewhere. Or some fatherly advice. What's your poison?"

See? Cool Dad. I stand up, shaking my head. "Just tell me how one girl can make me act like a psycho, then I'll be on my way."

"You know, I'm still trying to figure that out."

***

"Three of Hearts." Hayles grabs my wrist, whipping it around so she can take a glance at the card tucked in my hand. "Fart. I thought I had that one."

I chuckle and put the seven of spades back in the deck. "Okay, try again." Taking another card from the middle, I give her a wink before she closes her eyes and starts humming.

We've been at this for an hour. She caught me driving down her street and said her mom wasn't home, so I could 'come on in!' Weird. Didn't expect it, but hey, I took advantage of the rare opportunity.

She's gotten twenty-four cards right, five of which were in a row, telling me she has telepathic powers. I told her she's full of crap 'cause if she was, she wouldn't need me to write a freaking list for her. She slapped my arm and got the next three out of five cards right.

And who am I to tell her she's crazy when she keeps lucking out?

"Jack of diamonds."

I glance at the card in my hand. "Ooh, close."

"Hearts! I mean hearts! Jack of hearts!"

She's right, damn it. I tuck the card back in the deck and say, "Nope, sorry."

She gasps. "You little liar."

I give her a big grin, crossing my arms. "Well, you'll never know for sure, will you?"

"I *do* know for sure." She gives me that cute evil smile, and that's when it clicks. I whip my head around to the full length mirror sitting behind me. Darn girl's been cheating this whole time!

"Holy sh… crap."

She busts up, rolling to the floor and giggling into the very white carpet in her room.

"Took you long enough to figure out," she says between fits of laughter. I know I look like a damn idiot, but I'm laughing with her. Also trying not to touch her, but I want to do that wrestling thing girls and guys do when they tease each other. I don't want to piss her off though.

She sits back up, wiping the tears from her eyes. "Oh my gosh, that was great."

Screw it. I'm going in.

I grab the deck of cards and leap to her side of the room. She lets out a little yelp as I put my hand over her eyes. I'm not being tough or anything. She could easily slip out from underneath me, but she doesn't. She keeps laughing and asking 'What the wallowing weasels are you doing?'

"Okay smartie pants," I say grabbing a card and keeping it close to my chin even though my hand is still over her face. "What card am I holding?"

Her laughter subsides. She's still smiling, and so am I. Always around her.

"Um, six of clubs?"

"No way."

I drop my hand from her eyes and flip the card around. Maybe the girl is telepathic.

"Ha!" She grabs the six of clubs from my fingers and shakes her head. "What are the freaking odds?" She smiles and playfully pushes my chest. "I think someone owes me an apology."

"Oh no. You lucked out." I tap her nose because while she's letting me, I'm going to touch her.

She smiles and shoves me against the wall, tucking herself under my arm.

Did that just happen? Everything inside me jumps with her this close, cuddling with me. Chocolate smell and soft body pressed against mine. And I wasn't the one who did it. I was more or less a pillow she fluffed before collapsing on.

Hot damn!

"You still haven't told me…" Her voice shakes, and she starts fumbling around with the necklace I've got on. "What does your tat—?"

"Hayley!" The front door slams and Hayles' face loses all its color.

"Crap, crap, crap." She leaps from my arms and starts shoving me towards the window. "Sorry, Brody, you have to go. Like, now."

Nothing comes out my mouth. Millions of questions pile in my head but get clogged on their way out. I give her a quick hug before crawling through the open window, out onto the part of the roof underneath it. How I get down from here… yeah, haven't figured it out yet.

"Hayley?"

Crap. That voice is much closer now. I hop onto the next level up's ledge because I'm stupid and don't think to get off the roof altogether. There's no window or anything from up here, so I flatten myself over where I just climbed up, hoping I won't be here long.

"I'm in here, Mom."

I shouldn't listen. I should block it all out and give Hayles privacy, but I'm too afraid to loosen my death grip on the roof to cover my ears. Heights are not my thing, and I'm man enough to admit that.

"Guess what?!" Hayles' mom's voice isn't what I expected. I saw her fru-fru 'I'm too good for you' stare from the window and instantly thought English and high-pitched. Not Cruella Devil on crack.

"What are you doing home?" Hayley's voice is completely passive, nonchalant, like I wasn't in her room ten seconds ago. She's good.

"I couldn't wait to tell you. I finally got you an appointment with Yvonne!"

Ah, I'm slipping. I adjust so I'm not hanging off the edge.

"Um, who?"

"Don't you ever listen to me?" Something creaks, and I slip some more. "The health specialist. She said she can get you down to a size two in a year! Isn't that great news? I can finally introduce you to Daniel."

Who the hell is Daniel?

"Yeah, that sounds great."

If Hayles is going for the sarcastic 'great', she nailed it.

"Don't do that. You know how important this is to me."

Silence. I slip again.

"Your appointment is next Monday. If you are eligible, you'll be an official client and meet with Yvonne every Monday and Thursday. Try not to be a lost cause. This is our chance to make you… better."

I hear Hayles' bedroom door shut seconds before I lose my grip and fall flat on my back on the ledge outside her window.

Ouch.

"Oh my gosh, Brody! Are you okay?" She's whispering, but her face is crazy frantic.

"Uh huh."

"Sorry, I thought you'd hop down onto the shed."

Yes. That would've been the smart thing to do.

"It's okay." I sit up and rub the back of my neck. I'll be sore tomorrow.

"I'd invite you back in, but…"

I throw her a smile and a shrug. "Don't worry about it. I'll see you at school."

"Okay."

Eyeing my target, which is the shed about four feet down from where I'm at, I get ready to jump, but her voice stops me.

"You didn't… you didn't hear that did you?"

I'm about to tell her the truth. Her mom is dead wrong about whatever it is because Hayles doesn't need to get 'better.' She's already perfect. But Hayles' face looks terrified. Worse than the nervous face the other day at the tatt parlor. Worse than when she told me about that punker, Jason. Worse than the look she gave me on Friday when I told her I wanted to be with her.

How can I tell her I overheard something she didn't want me to? Something I had no right to know until she was ready to tell me? Something I'm still a little confused about?

I can't. So I lie.

"Hear what?"

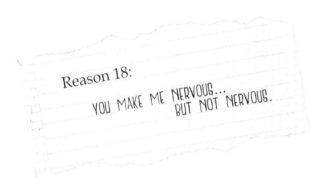

Reason 18:
YOU MAKE ME NERVOUS...
BUT NOT NERVOUS.

"Andy Grammer."

"Hmm…" I flip through the choices on the iPod. "Fine by Me?"

Hayles takes a sip of her Pepsi and mashes the earbud farther in her ear. "That's two for you." It's technically three, but she didn't count when I guessed Snow Patrol, because I said Snow Police, but she knew what I was talking about. "Gosh, do you have everything on here?"

Passing the iPod to her, I say, "You won't find your precious Katy Perry."

"Okay, then explain to me how the heck you knew every word on our date."

Shoulda kept my mouth shut. "Uh, a friend used to listen to a lot of that shit." Whoops. "I mean crap."

She raises her eyebrow. "Was this friend a girl?"

"Why do you assume that?"

"'Cause you've got that look on your face like you don't want to tell me 'cause you think I'll get jealous or something." She nudges my shoulder. "Plus, what guy listens to Katy Perry with his bro buddies?"

I chuckle. "Good point."

We sit and listen to "Fine by Me" which is still more popish than I'd like. Quynn was the one who put it on my playlist, and I kept it on there 'cause of the words and junk. For some reason I thought it meant something. Now as I'm listening with Hayles, it *does* mean something.

It's raining again today, and I'm waiting with her in the doorway for her mom to show up. I offered a ride—I'm not being a jackass today, but she kept shrugging me off. Darn stubborn girl.

"Can I ask you something?" Duh, I just did.

She nods, sticking a piece of gum in her mouth and offering me the package.

Damn it, I'm shaking. Didn't know it till I slid the gum out, and I couldn't get the wrapper off.

"You busy this weekend?"

How can this girl get me so nervous and not nervous at the same time? Her forehead crinkling like she's confused I want to spend time with her. Her big eyes blinking so fast like she's not sure I'm real. Then her chest flushing—because I can't help myself by looking at her all the time—like the simple thing of me asking her if she has plans, that I care about what she's up to, gets her flustered.

She's got me hooked, but does she even know?

No. She doesn't. She thinks she's a cow who doesn't deserve to be thought about the way I'm thinking about her. If that makes sense.

'Course it doesn't. She's made me insane.

"Nothing. Why?"

"Because you never answered me on Friday."

"About…?"

"About going out with me again. So I thought I'd give it a shot." Man, I'm not doing this right. I sound like a major dick. That it won't matter if she says yes or no because I couldn't give a crap.

But I give a whole lot more than a crap.

"Will you make my day and say you'll go out with me again on Friday?" Gag-worthy line, but screw it. I'll lay on the cheese if it'll make her clue in.

She rolls her eyes and nudges me with her elbow, then shocks the crap out of me by resting her head on my shoulder.

"I really wish I could, Brody, but Friday's not good for me."

Boo.

"Oh, okay."

Her body pulses, and I think it's 'cause she's cold her something, then I realize she's laughing.

"I'm not saying 'no'. Can we just go out Saturday instead?"

I seriously almost fist pump the air. Instead I try to play the cool guy card and end up mumbling some incoherency about how she's awesome and stuff. Ugh.

Some big gold SUV pulls up and judgmental mom looks at me and Hayles like we've been puked on or something. Hayles jumps off my shoulder and drops her books as she fumbles to get them in her bag.

I crouch down and help her. When she stands and shoulders her backpack, I go in for a hug, but she ends up doing this handshake thing that's completely awkward.

"Um, call you later."

"Sure." Better make sure my phone isn't on silent. "See ya."

Can't help but watch her walk away. She plops in the front seat, and I hear Crack Cruella's voice tell her to be more graceful or some crap like that. Hayles hides her face with her hair and doesn't give me a second glance as they drive off. I can hear her mom lecturing the whole way out of the parking lot.

Sometimes I wish it was okay to punch a grown woman.

***

I'm like a damn girl taking out the phone every five minutes like somehow the action will magically make it ring. I'm also stupid enough to try to send out mind waves in the direction of her house saying, 'Call Brody. Call Brody.' Telepathic my ass.

Then it hits me and I whack myself in the forehead. She had that appointment with Yazzie or something. The health specialist. No wonder she was a tiny bit off today. Not letting me take her home, playing games but not smiling her Hayley smile, and not even a flinch when I swore.

Is there anything I can say? Do? Dude, I'm not even supposed to know about it.

"You all right there?"

Dad leans against the door frame, Mom punching him in the gut. He pretends like it really hurts when it probably didn't even make a dent. She rolls her eyes, stalks over to the window and flings it open.

Huh. Thought I sprayed enough cologne to cover up the smell.

Mom's mumbling under her breath as she crosses the room. Her hands shove all my clothes I got piled on the bed before she sits next to me. "Don't know how he can live in this filth."

"I'm fine," I finally answer Dad. "You guys need something?" They rarely come to my room. You know, the smell and all. Now they're both here and it makes it feel like I'm in trouble.

"We just wanted to give you a heads up about our plans this week."

"And to make sure you'll be okay without us."

This week? Crap, is it Spring Break already?

Mom pats the spot next to her on the bed and I plop down, ready for the 'itinerary' since they'll force me to listen to it sooner or later.

"So, our plane leaves tomorrow afternoon. We were going to take a cab, but do you think you could drop us off?"

"Can we take the Dodge?"

Dad chuckles and air fist bumps me. "Yeah. You can borrow it while we're gone too, but only if you're picking up some hot ladies."

"Mark!"

"He knows I'm kidding."

We both laugh, and Mom mumbles something again, but I don't catch it.

"*Anyway*... we trust you, honey. Even with everything that happened with your brother, we know you'll be okay... not throw any wild parties or anything."

She makes it sound like I'm a saint. I smile and sling my arm around her shoulders.

"I may have game night here, but that's it. Just a few friends, a few beers, and some condoms for the orgy."

Dad busts a gut while Mom threatens to shove a tomato in my face.

"I told you, the boy will be fine."

"Really, Mom. It's not like you guys have never left town before."

The corner of her mouth twitches, and Dad's there in a second, sitting on the other side of her and grabbing her hand. I pull my arm off her shoulders, letting him be the one to do the comforting crap. She's Mom, and I'd do it, but she has him. And I'm glad she has him. He gives me a head nod 'cause he knows I get that.

"I just… if Gabe shows up…"

Ah, the douche brother is the problem.

"I'll control myself." I put my hand over my heart and the other out like I'm giving a bike signal. "No more busted noses or sore knuckles."

Instead of laughing, like I expect her to, like she normally would have, her eyes get shiny before she buries her face in her hands. I give Dad a look that says, 'What the hell?' He's rubbing her back, shushing her and shrugging at me.

"I just wish our family was… why can't we…?"

Dad smirks. "All just get along?"

Her laugh comes out like a rush of air, and she nods. "I know it's stupid."

"It's not stupid, Mom." 'Cause it's not. Our family shouldn't be so messed up. I wish I had that buddy-buddy thing with Gabe like I used to. I even wish Mark was my real dad… okay, he's my 'real' dad, but not my biological dad. And I wish Mom didn't have to deal with it all.

"I miss having Quynn around." She smiles and sort of nudges me. "Things were pretty good when she was, huh?"

Ah hell. This is the moment she chooses to tell me her obvious preference with the girls in my life? I get it. Mom and Quynn are like family. And things *were* awesome when Quynn was around. But she's not Hayley. I can't help but think if Mom knew Hayley, she wouldn't be shoving Quynn in my face every chance she could.

"I guess." That's all that comes out.

"Okay, enough of the heavy." Dad squeezes Mom's shoulders. "Let's talk about the fun stuff."

They give me a play by play on their plans this week, Dad winking at Mom every time they say they'll be 'sleeping'. Yuck. Basically, all I hear is they'll have a bunch of fun together, romance and all that other junk, and they'll be home on Sunday night. Oh, and I'm not allowed to have an orgy.

My phone rings right as Dad is giving Mom another wink, and I leap up to get it.

I thought only girls get all… what do they call it? Fluttery? Dude, I dunno, but crazy crap jumps up and down in my stomach when I see Hayles' name on the screen.

"You guys done making those gross faces? Can I…?" I hold up the phone and they both take the hint, Dad pinching Mom's butt on the way out.

Yes, it's gross 'cause it's my parents, but seeing them together, that's what love should be like, right?

That's sappy. I'm going soft.

"Hey. What's up?"

Silence. Nothing. Maybe I didn't get to it in time.

No wait. There's a hitched breathing or something.

"Hayles?"

Nothing again. Starting to freak me out. I'm already headed for the car keys.

"Can… can we go to the library?" she whispers.

"Yes." Car keys are now in my hand. Mom and Dad have already made it to their room. I'll text them or something. They probably want to be alone.

"I'm… I'm not at home."

"Where are you?"

She gives me an address, and I run to the kitchen to write it down.

134

"I'll be right there."

"Thank you."

"Hayles?"

"Yeah?"

"You okay?"

Silence again. Long enough that I'm in the car and pulling out of the driveway before she answers.

"Could you hurry?"

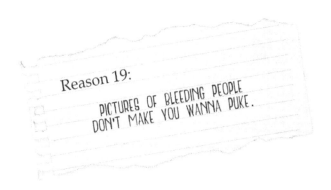

Reason 19:
PICTURES OF BLEEDING PEOPLE
DON'T MAKE YOU WANNA PUKE.

Even flying down the road at a speed I didn't know the Corsica was capable of, I don't get there as fast I want to. I leave the car running against the curb when I pull up, jump out and sprint to Hayles, who's sitting drenched in the rain at some decrepit building I've never been to or seen, just outside of town.

She doesn't say anything, and I don't either. Just tuck her into my arms and pull her inside the car.

More silence as I climb in next to her, turn up the heat and get her out of wherever it is we are.

I'm scared as hell to ask her what's up. She's not turning on the radio, or putting her feet on the dash, or even crying. She's being too quiet for Hayley, and nothing is coming to my mind about how to break the silence.

After a few minutes, I'm ready to slap on the stereo just to get rid of the tension in the air, but she finally says something.

"Thanks."

I glance at her before turning back to the road. She isn't looking at me. "Uh huh."

"You don't have to stay with me at the library if you don't want to."

I look at her again. She's looking at me, too.

"You still want to go to the library?" I attempt a smile. "Or do you wanna try some video games at my place?"

She laughs, but not a real one. "And risk another power outage?"

I shrug. "Sure."

Her lips press together and she looks back out the window. "Thanks, but I really just... I need to go to the library."

I sigh, turning onto the road that'll take me there. "Okay, but I'm not leaving you alone."

"Really, Brody, I can take the bus—"

"I'm not leaving you."

I know I probably sound like a dick, but I'm not going to just drop her off after... whatever it is that happened. She's blushing and smiling—a real one—still not looking at me, but I'll take whatever I can.

There's more silence during the rest of the drive, the walk into the library, and then more when we go back to the 'dead to the world' section. Then she breaks it by telling me to save the couch and she'll be right back.

I throw myself in the seat and kick my legs up to take over the whole thing so no one will sit next to me. Not like they would. Hayles comes back with a big fat book tucked against her chest.

She shoves my feet off the couch and sits cross-legged right next to me, letting me put my arm around her shoulders. She opens the book, and my eyes bug out of my skull.

"Uh..."

She giggles. "Yeah, this is what happens to the boys in the Amazon's Satere Mawé tribe when they become a man."

I choke back the bile rising in my throat, trying to be the macho man, but uh, yeah, not sure if I can handle Bullet Ant Gloves. The poor kid's hands are so swollen and red, they could be balloon animals. How Hayles is looking at this with a big grin on her face, I have no idea, but it makes me feel like a major pussy. I flip the page from the nasty looking fingers.

Oh man. The acrophobic in me also can't handle the kids

REASONS I FELL FOR THE FUNNY FAT FRIEND

hanging from their ankles by vines off of very large cliffs.

"This is called land jumping." Hayles smiles as she smoothes the page. "It says if their head doesn't touch the ground, it'll be a bad harvest."

"You mean, they have to bang in their skull?"

"Not if they're *really* careful." She winks and flips the page.

I take a deep breath and throw my head back against the cushion. "Okay, so why is that kid shoving an arrow into his tongue?" And why are you showing me this stuff?

Her butt slides closer to mine as she settles the book in my lap. All right, I don't understand what's going through her head—hate this picture gazing at me, but I can't help but feel like maybe this is what she needs to fix what's bothering her. To look at gross pictures and talk about crazy shit.

"Matausa tribe. They think if they get rid of the female blood in them, their mother's blood, then they'll attract more women and become braver."

"Yeah, that makes a whole lot of sense."

She laughs and shrugs against me. "You're looking green. Maybe I should put it away?"

"No." I get it. This is what she needs. "Keep going. It's fine."

She gives me another once over, in which I try to look comfortable, then she turns the page again.

"Holy crap! That kid is naked!"

"Shh!" She's laughing at me while pressing a finger to my lips.

"They have this stuff in the library?" I say under her hand.

"Yes. It's educational. And it's just a butt. I'm sure you've seen worse."

"No."

She shakes her head and rolls her eyes. "Cow jumping. They *have* to do it naked."

"How do you know all this stuff?"

Her hands graze over the page before she closes the book, leaving it in my lap. "I read it a lot."

I start running my hand up and down her arm. Her skin pops

with goose bumps, and I try to hide the smile forming on my lips. "Why? You into bizarre stuff like this?"

She doesn't look at me and keeps her eyes locked on the book in my lap. "I guess life just doesn't seem so bad sometimes when you see what these people have to do to please their parents."

Bingo. That's what it is. Her damn mom. I thought it might have something to do with the weird building and the frantic phone call.

I squeeze her shoulders, and her head falls onto my chest.

"Brody?"

"Yeah?"

"C-can I... can I hold your hand?"

I chuckle, don't mean to, but it comes out anyway. I grab her hand with my free one, the book clattering to the floor.

"You don't ever have to ask, Hayles."

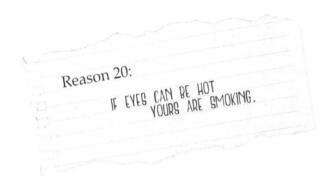

Reason 20:
IF EYES CAN BE HOT
YOURS ARE SMOKING.

Mom and Dad are gone. Whole week to myself, and I have nothing planned till Saturday. I'm a Class A loser.

And speaking of Saturday, I'm getting Hayles' list ready. I'm going to memorize it too because I'm not making more than one copy. My hand still hurts like hell, and I'm not going to type it 'cause, well, girls probably don't want that. They like the handwritten junk.

The list is easier now. After seeing her on Monday and the way she was just so, I dunno, strong but still needed me, everything is coming out so much better. She won't care if I sound stupid or whatever. She'll get it.

There's a knock at my front door. I groan as I tuck away the list in my back pocket and trudge upstairs to answer it. Probably some salesman or something. And if it's Gabe, I'll just slam the door in his face.

Whoever it is, they knock again.

"Okay, okay, I'm coming!"

I swing the door open, the sound of pounding rain reaching my ears. Quynn stands under her bright pink umbrella with a huge smile on her face and says, "Hey, Bro! What you up to?"

It takes me a second to wipe the shock from my face. Quynn knows Mom is out of town. She also told me at school that her

Spring Break was stock full.

I'm not a fan of the 'pop in' either, but I wave her through the door anyway. "Uh, not much. Just hanging out."

She shakes off her umbrella and sticks it in the entryway before closing the door shut behind her. I know she's comfortable here—I get it, but I'm not too happy when she plants her butt on the couch without really asking if she can stay. For some stupid reason, I make sure the list is secure in my pocket before sitting next to her.

"Thought you said you were pretty busy this week."

She shrugs. "I am. But it's rainy and I thought since we didn't get to talk last Friday..." Her voice drifts off as she studies my face. "Oh my gosh, I'm sorry. Did I totally interrupt you doing something?"

She goes to stand, but I put a hand on her arm stopping her. Not sure why, though. I don't want her to stay, but I don't want her to leave either.

Man, I thought I had this figured out.

"No, you didn't. Just surprised me." I attempt a smile. "So, how's your Spring Break?"

Lame. I suck at chit-chat.

"Pretty good so far." She tucks her feet under her butt and slides closer to me. I try to move away without being so obvious about it. "Parties the past couple nights. I was hoping to see you there, but someone thinks he's too good for that stuff." She shoves my leg and laughs.

I chuckle with her. Can't help it. "Nah, just not the party type. You know that."

She rolls her eyes. "Yes, I *know*. One of these days I'll get you to come with me." Her face goes bright red. "I mean go with me, not come..." She slaps her forehead while I laugh my face off. "Please change the subject before I die."

"Okay, when Mom and Dad gave me their itinerary for the weekend, they included every time they'd be... 'sleeping'."

Quynn perks up, face still red, but she's laughing. "Ew!"

"You're telling me."

"At least you know when not to call them."

We bust up, and I hop off the couch. "You want something to drink?" It's like it was before, funnily enough. Better actually because I'm not nervous around her. I see her, talk with her, but I'm not *wanting* her. It's kind of a relief.

"Sure, thanks." She grabs a blanket off the back of the couch and wraps it around her shoulders. It's the same blanket Hayley used when we played twenty questions, and just when I think I've got a grip on the situation, my heart does a funky knot thing. Not sure if Hayles would like me hanging with Quynn alone. Pretty sure that's a big no-no in convincing her she's the one I want.

And I'm not stupid. I know Quynn is flirting with me.

This is screwed up. I'm not like Gabe. I'm not like bio-dad.

But I'm not rude either, and I don't want to just kick her out.

All of this is going through my brain as I make like a robot and get us some Cherry Pepsi from the fridge.

"So, uh…" I stutter as I sit back down, in the recliner this time, "what do you got going on the rest of the day?"

Please say she has plans.

"Nothing! Totally wide open. Why? You want to do something?"

Ah hell.

"N-not sure if I can." *Complete lie, Brody. Just tell her the truth. You're seeing someone else.* "It's Friday night."

Again, that's my copout because I have no plans with Tanner at all. I'm such a wuss.

"Another game night." She sighs. "You should really go with me to Jamie's party tonight. I wasn't planning on going, but if you're there…"

Her eyes do that puppy dog thing. It sucks. Hayley does that too, but she doesn't ever mean to. Her eyes are just naturally big and round, suck-you-in green and innocent. They're hot eyes, if eyes can be hot. Maybe it's 'cause she smiles with them.

I shake my head and focus on Quynn, who is now chewing on her bottom lip.

Hayles never bites her lip. Only that once, and it was weird.

"I don't—"

"I'm not letting you say no." She points a finger at me. "You skip out on all the fun stuff. You're going and that's that."

She stands up, crossing her arms, giving me the 'I'm teasing but I'm serious about it too' look. She tosses her blonde hair over her shoulder and leans down, holding the arms of the recliner.

"Please, Brody?"

Girls suck. I don't like her like I used to—I know that for sure—but how do they have such power over guys? One word. That cursed word. *Please*. Ugh.

"I'm bringing Tanner."

She smiles and claps her hands together. "Point, Quynn."

I chuckle, but it's forced. Then she babbles on about parties or some other stuff. I'm not paying attention. All that's going through my stupid head is what Hayley will think if she finds out.

Oh! Maybe she'll come with me. I could text her right now!

No, wait. She said she had something going on tonight, which is why we're going out tomorrow.

Damn it.

But I will call Tanner. This will not be a date. 'Cause I'm over Quynn. I've got Hayles. Or at least, I want to have Hayles.

Then why can't I just spit out the words? Why can't I tell anyone? Not Mom or Dad, not Quynn. Not even Tanner knows. Only person who does is my douche of a brother, and that's 'cause he saw me with her. What's wrong with me?

"Okay, I'll see you later then!"

I must be on autopilot, 'cause I've walked her to the door and helped her with her jacket without even realizing it.

"Uh, yeah, okay."

She skips off the porch to her car, then waves at me as she drives off.

Yup, I'm a wuss.

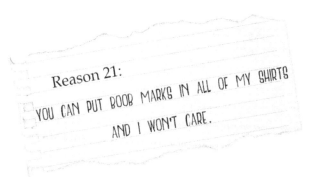

Reason 21:
YOU CAN PUT BOOB MARKS IN ALL OF MY SHIRTS
AND I WON'T CARE.

What do you wear to a party you don't want to go to? Nothing? Yeah, showing up buck ass naked will be a sure sign of, 'I'm not into you. Sorry if I led you on.' This stuff is messed up, I'm telling ya.

I called Tanner, but he didn't pick up. Sent him a text instead, which I'm sure shocked the crap out of him. Probably made him wonder if it was really me.

Then, just for the fun of it, I invited Hayles too. I know the answer will be no, but I'm kind of hoping her plans got changed or something. She hasn't said a word since I dropped her off—late—on Monday. No text, no calls… I may as well have had fifty conversations by myself.

I'm hoping we're at least still on for tomorrow. It'll be no tattoo parlor, but I've got my list ready for her.

I run my hand over my wrist before grabbing my wristband to cover up the tatt. I'm finally able to wear it again without it itching. Then I put on the first shirt and jeans that don't smell like butt and get out of my room. I've cleaned it—Mom will be proud—but I'm still in the midst of laundry. There were a lot of clothes under the bed. Among other things.

Grabbing the keys, I do a mental checklist of everything in the house. Back door, locked. Windows closed. Hall light on. No text from Hayles or Tanner. And fly… whoops, better zip that up.

All right, I'm done stalling. Better get this over with.

It's still raining. Pouring buckets as Dad would say. Nothing like living in the central point of God's showerhead.

And because I'm majorly pathetic, I take the long route to Jamie's house. I have to drive by Hayley's just to see if she's really not some sexually frustrated fantasy I've concocted over the past few weeks.

Nope, her house is still there. Lights out except for the porch light. Guess Hayles did have something going on tonight. Not that she'd lie about it, but I know she hides things from me.

I'm about to turn off the road when something in her driveway catches my eye. A shadowy figure crouched on the ground, shaking and trying to keep dry under the very little covering the garage has.

Holy shit.

I slam on the brakes and back up. Then I park the big truck against the curb. I'm texting and sprinting at the same time, telling Quynn I won't be there, then jamming my phone in my pocket before lifting a soaking wet chin up so her eyes meet mine.

"Hayles, what the h—?"

"B-Brody? What are y-you doing h-here?"

"Are you locked out?"

She nods, teeth chattering as her whole body goes into tremors.

"Why didn't you call someone?"

She tucks her hand in her pocket, pulling out her phone. "W-waterlogged."

Crap, is this what happened before?

"When will your mom be home?"

She shrugs… I think. She's shivering too much for me to tell. I grab her and pull her to her feet.

"Come on. I'm taking you to my house."

She doesn't argue, but she doesn't let me hold on to her either. She curls into herself and I can't be sure, because of the rain, but I think she's crying.

The heater's up all the way as I go back to my house, trying not to hydroplane. When we get there, she still won't let me touch her. Just walks alongside me and stands in my doorway while I run to get her a towel.

"You know what?" I say after trying to dry her off, and it not working at all. "Just go take a warm shower."

Her eyes flick up to meet mine. Those sexy eyes I've been thinking about. "Y-your p-parents w-won't m-mind?"

Wish she'd let me rub her arms. She's freezing. "They're not here. Please, go warm up."

"I-I don't h-have any e-extra clothes."

"You can borrow some of mine, and I'll stick yours in the dryer."

She rolls her eyes and attempts a smile. "I-I won't f-fit in y-your clothes."

"Knock it off." I go for her hand, but she pulls it out of my way. "Go take a shower, all right? I'll give you a sweater and some pants and I guarantee they'll be fine."

She shakes her head, but goes upstairs to the bathroom while I run and grab the cleanest stuff I can find.

"Here," I say as I open the door a crack to hand her my clothes. When I feel the weight off my arm I pull it back out and leave her to it. I hear a small 'thanks' before I get back downstairs.

This is the part where I speed clean. After getting into some dry clothes of my own of course. Living by myself for the past few days made the whole house try to do an ass room impression. I get the couch cleared off and the kitchen sink emptied, then hurry to my room to do a double check. And spray cologne all over it. Again, not like I'm expecting her to be in here, but what if she needs to stay the night? She can take my bed, and I'll sleep in Mom and Dad's. Or take the couch. No biggie.

I hear the water shut off just as I clear out the dryer so it's open for her clothes. She's going to be wearing my underwear, my sweater, no bra. Whoa, things are shifting around and I haven't even seen her yet.

And damn it, I can't be some horny jackhole right now. There's something really screwed up going on in her life, and she's going to tell me about it. Even if I have to force her into twenty questions.

"Hey."

She's got an arm wrapped around her chest and the other holding out her soggy clothes. The hoodie isn't tight, not baggy, but not tight, and the pants fit. I give her an 'I told you so' look before grabbing her stuff and throwing it in the dryer. The bra misses, hitting the floor, and I quickly pick it up by two fingers and chuck it in, slamming the door behind it. She's laughing at me as I start the dryer.

"It's just a bra."

"Yeah, yeah." I motion her to the couch. "You want something to drink?" Dude this sounds familiar. Was doing this with another girl not five hours ago. But it's different now.

"Something warm, please."

"'Course."

Only thing I got is apple cider. I call from the kitchen to make sure she's okay with that. She is, so I make two mugs and try to sit as close as she'll allow me to.

"Ooh, yummy. Thank you." She's smiling her Hayles smile and tugging at the hoodie.

"Is it itchy or something?" I point to her stomach where she's pulling the sweater away from her body.

"No, I just don't want to put boob marks in it." She laughs. "But I think it's impossible. It'll be a little stretched out in the chest region for you."

"You can keep it if you want," I say before taking a gulp of the boiling cider. My eyes water and I shut them as I try to push back the burn in my throat. She starts laughing.

"You know, you can sip that and I won't think you'll be any less of a man."

I push her leg and set the mug down. "Are you warm enough?"

She nods, blowing across her drink before taking a sip.

"All right, then, now is when you tell me what you were doing out in the rain like that."

147

It's amazing how just in the few weeks I've known her—really known her—I can tell when she's about to shrug off a question like it's no big deal. Her eyes go to the most boring thing in the room, and the corner of her lip tugs upward with her shoulder. She opens her mouth, to tell me the big lie she's got ready for me, and I cut her off.

"Hayles. I mean it." I take the cup out of her hands and put it on the coffee table next to mine. Sliding my fingers on her knee, I make sure she's looking at me before I say anything else. Takes a minute, but she finally locks gazes. "Don't hide this from me anymore. Something's wrong, and I can't stand to see you like this."

"Like what?" she whispers.

I press the crinkle between her eyebrows and smooth it out. "Scared."

A flicker of a smile crosses her face, and she holds my hand to her cheek. I know it's not the right time, but I'm leaning toward her anyway. Ready to press my lips to hers. To take away all the pain I know she's feeling but not telling me about. She's so beautiful. Even scared and sad like this.

I get close enough to taste her breath, then she drops my hand and turns, giving me her cheek.

I don't mean to growl, but I do.

She looks back at me, catching my face between her hands. "I'm sorry." She's not lying. "I want you to kiss me, I do."

"But...?"

Another flicker of a smile. "It's my first time kissing someone. I want it to... I want to make sure it really means something."

Ouch.

"It won't mean something with me?"

She drops her hands. "You mean more to me than you should. But, I *still* think you're hung on Quynn. I don't want to let you in only to have you run off with her."

My mouth hangs open. I'm pretty sure I look like a fool. Is this really what she thinks? I'll pull a Gabe?

I'm. Not. Like. That.

"You think I could do that to you?" Damn it, now I'm pissed. Not the time for it since there's something a lot worse bugging her. Still, it sucks she thinks that about me.

"Not on purpose."

I sit back as far as I can on the other end of the couch, shaking my head at my feet. "I don't understand, Hayles. I need you to tell me what's going on. Why you'd think I'd do that to you. Why you won't let *any*one in. Why you called me to pick you up on Monday. Why you were sitting in the rain. Why you don't want me to meet your mom." I bury my face in my hands. "I want to help, be there for you, but I can't if I don't know anything. I can't if you don't *let* me."

Yeah, I said that all out loud. Well, muffled into my fingers. I won't look at her, too afraid she's pissed and she'll just walk away, leaving me with the list in my pocket.

I hear a deep breath from the other end of the couch. Still won't look at her, and I can't tell if she's frustrated, hurt, or what, just off that sigh.

"She doesn't want me to meet him."

My eyebrows pinch together, and I glance at her through my hands. She's picking at a loose thread on the pocket of the hoodie. "What?"

"That's why I was sitting outside. My mom doesn't want me to meet Daniel until I'm... thinner."

I gulp, sitting up straight. "Who's Daniel?"

"Mom's boyfriend."

That small part of me that was worried about whoever this Daniel was whoops for joy in my stomach.

"So you were sitting in the rain because...?"

She throws her head against the cushion of the couch and talks to the ceiling. "She told me she was going to go over some menus and stuff with me tonight. She's making me see a health specialist. But Daniel pulled up and surprised her with a date. She shoved me outside, and I guess she forgot to leave the door unlocked when she left."

She sighs, tilting her head forward. Tears are forming at the outer corners of her eyes. "I didn't tell you because it's embarrassing. It just confirms what I've been trying to ignore."

"Which is what?"

"That I'm not good enough for anyone. I'm too... big to have someone like me the way you say you do."

The tears finally spill over, and she quickly swipes them away. I scoot closer to her again, taking it all in. All the pieces coming together about why she looks at herself the way she does. I had no idea it was so bad. 'Cause she never told me.

"On Monday, I had my first appointment with the health specialist. She told my mom I needed more exercise, you know, the same old crap they all say. Well, my mom thought it would be good for me to walk home. So she took me to where you picked me up, and left me there. Said if I didn't get home within an hour, I wouldn't get dinner." She chuckles, but it sounds off. "It's like I'm five."

I shake my head. "That's messed up." I know I should say something better than that, but she laughs and swipes another tear from her face.

"So, I called you because, well, you saw that place! It was freaking scary! And who cares if I got dinner that night? It was probably a glass of water and a broccoli floret."

She's laughing now, but still crying. I know I'm pushing my boundaries when I clasp her wrist and guide her onto my chest. She goes, but hesitantly.

"I'm sorry you have to deal with this crap." *So eloquent, Brody.* "For the record, I don't think you need to see a health specialist. I don't think you need to change anything about you. You're...you're perfect."

She traces the design on my shirt, not saying anything.

"And... uh..." I gulp. "Thanks."

She looks up at me. "For what?"

"Trusting me enough to tell me all of that."

Her face goes back into my armpit. "Can I ask you a silly question?"

I let out a breathless chuckle. "Sure."

"You don't mind touching me?"

Man, I want to touch her more. "That *is* a silly question," I say, squeezing her. "I feel like I'm trying to grope you every time we're together."

We laugh together, her head jiggling around on my stomach.

"Why would you think I minded?"

"Well, 'cause I'm probably, uh, squishier than most girls."

Darn girl.

"You know, whenever you let me touch you, even when it's just like this, laying on my chest, you make me feel like I've won some sort of prize. You need to stop being so self-conscious, Hayles. I *love* touching you."

She shrugs out of my grasp, and I get real confused for a second, 'cause I thought I nailed that one. Then she leaps on top of me, straddling me and hugging me around my neck.

Holy hell, this is happening! I knew I nailed it!

I wrap my hands around her waist, pulling her closer to me. We're both laughing, and I'm not sure why. Her laugh just makes me laugh.

We sit there for a while, talking and she keeps herself planted on my lap. My legs are falling asleep, and I'm not all that comfortable, but who cares? She asks where my parents are, and I tell her the embarrassing display I was witness to. She laughs and tells me she likes my parents already. Like she's planning on meeting them someday. Someday soon. I like that. Makes things between us seem more real. She's starting to get it.

The dryer buzzes, and that's when I stumble off the couch to get her clothes. I'm stomping my feet a little harder than I normally do to get rid of the pins and needles in my legs.

I hand Hayley her clothes, and she hesitates. "Can I change in your room?" Her face is bloodshot.

"Sure." She can today, since it's clean. I lead her downstairs, then give her privacy after she makes fun of the swimsuit calendar I have on the wall. I'm putting the mugs in the sink when she comes back upstairs.

"I should probably head back home." She smiles, but it doesn't go up to her eyes. Yeah, I don't want her to leave either.

"I'll give you a ride."

There's some kind of awkward tension in the air as I grab the keys and open the door. She pauses in the doorstep, back towards me.

"You okay?"

She nods and turns around, pushing her eyes up to meet mine. "Do you... I mean, you don't think I'm too f—"

"If you say the word 'fat' one more time I'm going to knock you upside the head." I lean against the doorknob, watching the rain fall behind her. "You gotta stop believing your mom. She's wrong. And if she's too embarrassed by you, then she's not worth pleasing. You're her daughter. That should be good enough." I pause to tuck a strand of hair behind her ear. I'm not afraid to touch her anymore. "You *are* good enough. At least I think so."

She smiles her Hayley smile. Then she glances over her shoulder at the pouring rain. I really don't want her to go, but if she thinks her mom's going to be home, I don't want to get her in trouble either.

Her head whips back around, scaring me a little. The smile is still on her face, but she looks kind of nervous. And when she says something, I know why.

"Kiss me."

Reason 22:
YOU SMILE WHEN YOU KISS.

Wait. What did she just say? "Huh?"

"I want you to kiss me now." Her lips pull up into that amazing smile, and she lets out a nervous giggle.

"You… you sure?"

She nods and takes a step closer. I can't believe she's saying this to me now. After all that stuff with her mom and after the whole, 'I want my first kiss to mean something', I didn't think she'd be ready for it… now. I mean, thought I'd have to wait at least a couple of days.

I gulp and close the distance between us. Man, I hope I do this right. Don't want to make her first kiss too slobbery or awkward or anything that'll disappoint her. She deserves to have a kiss that'll make her want more. A kiss that'll tell her exactly how I feel about her.

Cupping her face between my hands, I gauge her eyes before I go in farther. She closes them and lets out a small puff of air I can taste. Her mint chocolate smell makes me close my eyes too, and I pull her closer, noses touching, breath mixing.

"Um, Brody?"

The air rushes out of my lips, which are centimeters away from hers. "Yeah?"

"Can you like, not use your tongue?"

Can't help the chuckle that rumbles through my throat. "What?" We both open our eyes, but I keep her face close.

"It's just, I already don't know what the crap I'm doing, and if you stick your tongue in my mouth, I really don't know how I'm going to... like, I don't know how that all works, so if you could keep it to yourself this first time around—"

"Hayles," I interrupt. Darn girl is going a million miles a minute. "I won't use my tongue, I promise."

She sighs, her breath smacking me in the face again. "Okay, sorry." She smiles. "Continue."

I'm about to, taking my time again to relish the fact I'm freaking going to kiss my girl, noses touching again, hands on her soft cheeks...

"Brody?"

I sigh, but it sort-of comes out like a growl. "Yeah?"

"Sorry," she says, pulling back. Wait, did she change her mind? No, she's smiling and kind of giggling. "So, like, what if I'm bad at this?"

"What?"

"You'll tell me if I'm bad at the whole kissing thing, right?" She reaches up and rubs her temples, closing her eyes tight. "Or at least you won't judge me too harshly for not knowing where to put my hands or how to move my lips or anything."

"Hayles," I say, pulling her back toward me, "don't over-think this, 'kay?"

She takes a deep breath, grabs my hands and sticks them back on her cheeks. "Okay, sorry." Her eyes close. "Give it to me."

I chuckle, shaking my head. Girl is so amazing. How did I end up being the lucky first guy to give her this moment? I'm still smiling as our lips barely touch.

"Um..."

Ugh! This girl!

"What is it now?"

"Did I... gosh, did I put too much pressure on you?"

"What?"

"'Cause I didn't mean to. You're not worried about it, are you? Like, this is what you wanna do, right? You still *want* to give me my first kiss? Or am I just pressuring you into it? Or is there too much pressure now to make it perfect, 'cause Brody, it doesn't have to be. I want it to be you 'cause you're frigging fantabulous and I like you so much and I didn't mean to, like fall so hard for you. It just happened and now I have no idea how this is supposed to go and if you even feel the same way you felt last week when you told me you were, like falling for me too or if you just feel bad 'cause of my mom and all that junk. I mean, you haven't even given me any reasons yet and I'm not sure if it's 'cause you couldn't think of them or if you were just trying to be nice or—"

"Hayles!"

She stops her blabbering, snapping her lips tight together and getting a little flushed. I'm smiling so she is too, but this girl needs to put on her perception glasses.

I take a deep breath, wrap one arm around her waist so she doesn't go anywhere again, and brush her hair back with the other.

"Give me five numbers between one and twenty."

"What?"

"Just do it."

She cocks her head and lets out a tiny laugh. "Okay, one, three, eight, fourteen, and, um, fifteen."

Okay...

"Reason one..." I smile. "You know how to sign the word *balls.*"

Her mouth splits open, letting out a beautiful laugh.

"Reason three. You know how to make awkward, less awkward."

She cocks her head to the side. "How do I—"

"Reason eight." I'm cutting her off before she has any other chance to get away from me. "You slaughter me at Ghost Recon."

Another laugh. And she's getting closer to me. Her lips are almost against mine.

"Reason fifteen." I pull her shirt down a little to touch her shoulder blade. I feel her skin rise with goose bumps as I trail my finger tip across her tattoo. "That's a sexy tatt. And you know it."

She lets out another puff of air I can taste. "You missed fourteen."

Her smile is so huge and so beautiful, I want to push my lips against hers now, but I give her the last one. She needs to hear it, no matter how cheesy it comes out.

"Reason fourteen." I press my forehead against hers, locking her in my gaze. "You are so beautiful. Inside and out. I don't just need you. I *crave* you. Everything about you. You are the only person I've felt this way about. You're my best friend."

She lets out a small laugh, then runs her tongue across her bottom lip. "Brody?"

"Yeah?"

"I'm in trouble."

I chuckle. Her nose is touching mine again.

"Why is that?"

"I'm pretty sure I'm falling in love with you."

Holy hell. She beat me to it.

"I'm pretty sure I'm falling in love with you, too."

She smiles and tugs the sides of my shirt to pull me in. I don't need the hint though. I've been waiting for this moment for what seems like forever.

I make sure the first touch is soft, in case she wants to pull back, but when she doesn't, I lean into it so the kiss is harder. She's gotta know just how much I'm falling in love with her.

Better be careful though. I know she said no tongue, and I'm trying real hard not to taste her, even just a little bit. But I want to. I want to open my mouth to let her in. I want her to open hers to let *me* in. But I have to make this perfect for her. Exactly what she wants, and what she needs it to be.

She's still smiling, even though our lips are pressed tight. It's so awesome 'cause it's still Hayles. Even her kiss is full of life and just… awesomesauce.

Her hands haven't moved from my shirt, but they keep tugging on it, like she wants me closer. I can't get any closer than I already am. Bodies together, one hand cupping her face, the other… oh, I'm pulling her waist closer to mine too.

She starts to giggle a little bit through the kiss, her mouth opening enough for me to taste her, but I hold back. I'm not going to ruin her first kiss by doing what she told me not to. Don't even care that she's laughing during this. It's just Hayles. Who she is, and it's perfect.

Then the tip of her tongue touches my bottom lip. Did I imagine that? Oh no, I didn't, 'cause she does it again. And again.

Dammit, what is this girl doing to me?!

I open my mouth and meet her tongue with mine this time. Who cares if she pulls away. I'm blaming her for starting it.

She doesn't. She… she moans. Her hands slither up my chest and wrap around my neck, pulling me closer into her mouth.

Yeah, there's no way this kiss is ending. I can't get enough of her now that I have her. My hands move her waist so I can shut the door. I don't break the kiss—never going to if I can help it—and then I trap her against the wood.

She's smiling again. Still kissing me and smiling. And I'm taking every opportunity I can to keep tasting her. To feel her hands move around the back of my neck. To feel the skin on her waist as I lift her shirt and touch her pant line. She *is* soft. Beautiful and soft.

She's the first to break away, catching her breath and freezing in the position I have her in. I'm leaning toward her, using the door to keep me stable. I'm pretty sure I'm about to faint.

"Frigging f-bombs of glory."

I laugh. It comes out all breathless and junk. "Is that a good thing?"

She opens her eyes, flicking them up to meet mine.

"Can I have another one?"

Chuckling again. Right before I give her what she wants. She can ask me that anytime, and I'll give it to her. That was the best kiss I've ever had.

I keep her against the door, but she's moved her hands to the bottom of my shirt. She's hesitant in her actions, but I'm not sure if it's 'cause I'm distracting her with my mouth or not. Then her fingertips are grazing the skin by my bellybutton, and I let out an involuntary groan, breaking away from her lips and moving to her neck.

"Is… is this okay?" she asks, trailing her fingers across the lines on my stomach.

Hell yeah, that's okay.

"Uh huh," I breathe against her collar bone.

She keeps playing with my skin, moving to my sides and giving me goose bumps and doing other things to me I never thought I could feel with someone. There's some crazy stuff going on in my chest.

I press my lips against hers again, trying to keep my hands near her face 'cause if she keeps touching the skin underneath my shirt, I don't know what's going to stop me from doing the same to her. But I'm pretty sure since it took her so long to let me kiss her, this isn't going any further than…

Wait. Is she…? Yeah, she's trying to get my shirt off.

I pull back and gauge her eyes. She's smiling, blush in her cheeks and a look that asks, 'Is *this* okay?'

The biggest grin plants itself on my lips and I reach back, grab the neck of my shirt, and tug it over my head.

I've never been this naked with a girl before. I'm not self-conscious or anything, but it is different. Not weird. I'm definitely all right with Hayles seeing this much of me.

"Wowza."

Okay, now I'm a little embarrassed. "Is *that* a good thing?"

She puts her hands on my chest and her face goes from pink to red. "Why in the heck does someone like *you* want someone like *me*?"

She's crazy. I just told her she's the most beautiful person I've ever met, and she still looks at herself like she's butt ugly or something.

"Hayles—"

"Did I ever tell you I *love* it when you call me that?" Her eyes move from my chest to my face. "I've never had a nickname before."

I let out a breath through my nostrils, taking one of her hands in mine. "Hayles, you are gorgeous, all right. No more of this stuff about you being anything less than that."

She grins like she doesn't believe me, but she's not going to argue. I roll my eyes before I give her another long kiss. She's moved her hands back around my neck, giving me opportunity to play with the skin on her stomach.

"Is this okay?" I ask between kisses.

She hesitates, long enough for me to worry about what's going through her head, but then she nods. "Yes, but… I'm not, I mean, I'm sorry I'm not as skinny… you deserve someone who—"

"I want *you*." Because I do. I want everything with her. And I didn't expect our first kiss leading to this. I'm not sure if she did either, but I'm not going to stop until she tells me to stop. I love her. And I want to have one of my firsts with her too.

Taking the bottom of her shirt I slowly lift up. She's not telling me to stop, not even with her eyes. I can tell she's worried about what I'll see underneath, but she won't stop me.

So I'm not going to stop.

And holy hell. I'm glad I didn't.

Bra and jeans are the best look for this girl. Her curves, her breasts, her hips… I hold her body close to mine, skin on skin, and kiss her again. I don't stay at her mouth, though. I trace every inch of her neck, her collar bone, her cleavage, her stomach, her sides, even gliding my tongue across her skin to taste every bit of her. Because I *have* to. She's so gorgeous, this girl. She's letting me look, touch…

And she's not stopping me.

She pulls my face back to hers, kissing me with so much force I can't believe we're going this far. When she said 'kiss me' earlier, I was going to give her the kiss I'd been preparing for. Now I'm completely out of my element here. Going places I've never experienced before either.

I press my hips into her, making the door creak.

REASONS I FELL FOR THE FUNNY FAT FRIEND

"Whoa!"

"Sorry," I say, backing up and taking the chance to calm my breathing… and myself. I pushed too far. Dammit. I really didn't want to ruin this.

"No, it's okay." She laughs and brings a hand to her chest. My eyes rest there for a second before I force myself to look at her face and not her boobs.

"I'm sorry," I say again.

"Brody…" She giggles and grabs my hand. "It's. Okay. You just surprised me, that's all."

"S-sorry." Guess that's the only thing my mouth is capable of saying right now.

"Don't be sorry. I… I just didn't know I had that, um, effect on you."

Now I'm the one laughing. I shake my head and pull her to me, skin on skin again. I wrap my hand around the back of her head while I caress the small of her back with the other. I'm never letting her go.

I rest my cheek against hers so I can whisper in her ear. "You've had this effect on me since the day I saw you with that book on your head."

Feeling her smile against my cheek, I kiss under her earlobe and pull back. But she doesn't let me go far. Her fingers tuck into my belt, hands shaking a little as she starts to undo the buckle.

"I-Is this…" She gulps. "Okay?"

We both freeze as I stare into her eyes. It's okay with me… more than okay with me, but I have to make sure this is what she wants.

"Is it okay with you?"

She nods, a big smile forming on her lips.

As much as I want her to keep going, for us to keep going, I can't. I have to know…

"Why?"

"What?"

I grab her fingers, stopping her from getting too far downward.

160

Because once she does, that'll be it for my control.

"Why is this okay with you?" I let go of one of her wrists, and use the back of my hand to stroke her cheek. "Don't get me wrong, I want this—really want this—but you've been so careful physically with me. Why now? Why me?"

Another big smile plants itself on her face, but she looks nervous, too. And her voice comes out a little shaky. "I-I never thought I'd f-feel this way about anyone." Her eyes go to the floor, and I tilt her chin up so I can still look at the beautiful greens. She takes a deep breath. "I never really allowed myself to feel anything for anyone. But then you just... well, POP! There you were, and made me get all weird inside."

I chuckle and she laughs. She has no idea that's exactly how I felt when she... POP, came into my life.

"And well, besides the obvious reasons—"

"Obvious?"

She cocks an eyebrow. "Seriously? Brody, this is totally another reason why you're just super fabulous."

Huh?

"You don't even know how freaking hot you are. That's uber sexy." Her eyes go to my bare torso. "Count with me." One finger strokes part of my stomach. "One..." She moves an inch or two over. "Two..." She slides down. "Three..." Back over. "Four..." Down. "Five..." Over. "Six."

She flicks her gaze back up to me. "That's what people call a six-pack."

I roll my eyes, but she keeps moving her fingers up to my chest. I want to stop her, but I don't at the same time. It feels too good.

"And these..." She flattens her hands on me, and I tug her closer. "Are called pecs. It's like you stepped out of a fantasy."

I open my mouth, but her fingers zoom up to cover my lips. "How many girls have seen you like this?"

"One. Including you."

She smiles, resting her head on my chest. I run my hands up her bare back, wishing it was the right moment to undo that bra.

"Not even girls at a pool?" she whispers.

I shrug. "I'm not much of a swimmer."

Her hold tightens around my middle. That bra clasp teases my fingertips, so I move my hand upward to the back of her neck instead to keep control.

"That was the obvious reason," she says, looking at me again, "but you… you look at me like…"

A gust of air goes out her nose as she loses the words. I press my forehead against hers.

"Like you're the most gorgeous girl I've ever seen?"

She nods, and we're both quiet for a minute. Then I say, "What did I do to deserve you?" at the same time she says, "I don't deserve someone like you."

We chuckle and her fingers slide up to my neck. "It took me so long to let you kiss me because I knew this might happen."

That makes one of us. "You did?"

She nods again, keeping her dark green eyes locked on mine. "I knew once we started kissing, I wouldn't want to stop. And I don't." She sets her forehead on mine, then whispers against my lips. "Please, don't stop, Brody." Her fingers go back to my belt while my head spins. "I want to give you everything… if you want it."

Oh man, do I want it. I smile and hold her close, letting her undo my buckle.

"On one condition."

She pauses and looks at me. I kiss the tip of her nose.

"You let me give everything to you."

She gets my belt undone and whips it out from my belt loops. "Deal."

Her fingers go to my top button, and that's when I realize something that's pretty important.

"Wait… I don't think I have any protection, Hayles."

Her smile doesn't fall.

"You don't need to worry about that."

She twists my top button open.

"What?"

162

Her hands trail downward, and I'm about to lose all train of thought.

"It's a long story, and I promise I'll tell you." She kisses my neck as she gets my zipper down. "But later. I really don't want to ruin the moment with, uh, girly talk. Just know you don't have to worry about knocking me up."

Where did this confident Hayley come from? She's being so... seductive and sexy and yeah, I can't think anymore. I don't want to. I just want to be with her.

And give her another first as she gives me one of mine.

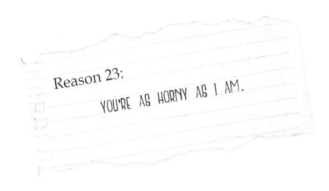

Reason 23:
YOU'RE AS HORNY AS I AM.

Mom and Dad couldn't have picked a better weekend to be out of the house. Waking up with Hayles in my arms is something that makes my gut clench in that good way.

She's still asleep... I think. There's a small smile on her lips from what I can see, but her back is to me. I kiss that sexy tatt on her shoulder, and she sighs.

Guess she is awake.

"Hey."

She sighs again. "Sup?"

I chuckle, tightening my hold on her waist. She tucks one of her legs between mine and giggles.

"What?"

Her neck twists so she can meet my eyes. "Jumping jellybeans, Brody. I'm just so frickin happy."

Ah hell. "Me too."

We kiss, I don't even care we both have morning breath. I got mints in my drawer if we need 'em. But I'm not moving from this spot until I have to.

"So, you're okay with... everything?"

She wiggles her body so she's facing me, hitching her leg up on my hip and grabbing my hand to put on her butt.

"I kinda wanna do it again." Her face flushes.

Sweet. 'Cause I want to do it again too. That was pretty much the best thing I've ever experienced.

"All right." Why is my voice shaking? I don't have any more reason to be nervous around her. She's given me everything already.

"Oh!" she squeals right as I go in for another kiss. "What time is it?"

I sigh. "Really?"

"Yeah." She leans up and searches the room for a clock. "Sorry, but I need to be home by... Crapola! Is that clock right?"

I should lie so she stays in bed with me. But I don't want any more trouble for her. "Yeah."

Her lip juts out as she cuddles back into me. "I gotta go."

No. "Just stay a little bit longer?" I tug her closer to my body, and I feel her sigh of defeat against my chest.

"Two minutes. But then I really have to go."

"I think we can pump one out in two minutes." I smile and tilt her chin up. She's laughing and smacks me... okay, more like taps me in the arm.

"As romantic as that sounds..." She rolls her eyes. "That's not what I meant. I just... can you just hold me?"

Hell yeah I can hold her. I'll even kiss her too.

"Hey," I say after what's been way longer than two minutes, "you promised me you'd tell me that long story about why, you know, we don't have to worry about, uh, protection."

"Oh that's right."

She's quiet, stifling a large grin as she traces patterns on my chest.

"So...?"

"I don't really have time to tell you, but you deserve to know I guess. Especially since we're probably going to be doing this a lot." Her eyes go to mine, her mouth popping open like she just realized she said that out loud.

She's so damn cute.

I kiss her, keeping my tongue in my mouth this time though in case of morning breath and not being able to control myself again, but it's hard and urgent enough for her to know that yeah, I want to do this with her forever.

When we break apart, she wraps her arm around my side and squeezes me close to her. "Okay, so you know the whole dairy theory, right?"

What the hell? "No."

She smiles and gives me a rapid nod. "Yeah! There was this awesome article about if you have a lot of dairy right before you have sex it works as a good birth control."

Oh no. She better be joking. But her eyes are dead serious, and she squeezes me again.

"And I had like, a ton of milk, two thingys of yogurt, and grilled cheese yesterday. So we should be good!"

No. No. No.

"Hayles…"

She busts out in laughter, her body pulsing against me and it's my turn to smack—more like tap—her in the arm.

"Ha. Ha. Ha. You think you're so funny." I smile and press my forehead against hers. "Will you please tell me the real reason now?"

"Okay, but the real reason has to do with a whole bunch of girly stuff you'll think is nasty."

"Try me." 'Cause after that dairy thing, I better make sure we were really 'covered' last night.

"I've been on the pill for like, two years now."

Okay…

"Why?"

"Girl stuff." She shakes her head. "Don't worry about it."

Don't worry about it? How can I not worry about it?

"But last night… it was your first time, right?"

"Duh."

"Then why—"

"Seriously, Brody. You don't want to know."

I wiggle my nose against hers. I probably don't wanna know, but I hate when she keeps things from me. "Come on."

She cocks her head, giving me the 'you asked for it' grin. "Okay, boy I'm in bed with, I used to have a high flow period and it was so bad I needed to be put on birth control so I don't go through a hundred tamp—"

"Okay!" Ugh, she was right. I didn't want to know. "I got it."

Her laughter is so contagious, even though she just about made me puke.

"Alrighty, close your eyes."

My eyebrow goes up. "Why…?"

"'Cause I have to get dressed." She tugs the blanket around her chest as she slides to the edge of the bed.

"And I have to close my eyes because…?" I saw everything last night, and yeah I want to see her again.

"Because things look different in the light." She smiles before putting her hand over my eyes. "And I don't want you going, 'Yuck! *That's* what I did it with last night?'"

Is she serious? "Knock it off, Hayles," I say, pushing her hand away. "You. Are. Beautiful." I reach over to tug the blanket off her, but she fights me.

"Hey!" She's giggling, and I take that as my cue to pin her against the mattress. Holding her arms above her head, I take in all of her while she's laughing and yelling at me to stop ogling.

I can't though. She's too hot.

"Hayles?"

She stops laughing, but the smile is still on her face. "Yeah, perv?"

My eyes go to hers. I don't even have to fight to keep them there. I want to look at her like this.

"Did you mean what you said last night?"

"Which part?"

Her hands slide from under my grasp and she rests them on my chest. It feels so good to be this close with her.

"That you're falling in love with me."

She reaches up and pulls the back of my neck so I can meet her lips. Yeah, this is the first time she's kissed me. She kissed me back a lot last night… but yeah, this is the first time she's made the move.

"Yes, I meant it," she says when we break apart. "Did you?"

I give her a sort-of smile. "No."

Her eyebrows scrunch together in that awesome way and I can tell she's about to yell at me, so I cut her off.

"I'm not falling in love with you." I give her a full smile this time, wiping her hair from her face. "I *am* in love with you."

She rolls her eyes and smiles. "Cheeseball."

I laugh and kiss the tip of her nose. "Well, I mean it. I love you."

I know I shouldn't expect to hear it back. She already did sort-of say it to me, but when she just sighs and tells me she's gotta go, my gut feels like she just socked it with a brick.

***

There's this scene on this chick flick Quynn made me watch with her once. That dude in Inception sleeps with that girl on Elf and he does this musical number thing walking down the street. I thought it was pretty fruity. No guy would act like that even if he did just score.

I'm now eating my words. I kind of want a whole bunch of people dancing in the background as I make my way to the Dodge, as I run to the store to get a bunch of junk food, as I go to the park 'cause I just wanna. I want to fist pump the air and skip and all that stuff, and I do a few times, then catch myself.

And from her reaction this morning, Hayles seemed pretty okay with everything. It was good for her, you know? She said she wanted to do it more. Not just again, but over and over again. That's damn hot. I *owned* it. Not that she had anything to compare it to, but she didn't say it was bad.

She wanted more.

Hell yeah!

I'm doing this weird jig as I walk up my porch, and I'm humming under my breath, something I never do. Look what this girl has done to me!

"You are in *big* trouble."

"Dammit!" I yell as I trip off the porch, dropping the bag of chips in my hand. Quynn stands up from the patio chair we've got in front of our window and crosses her arms.

"I'm not even going to apologize for scaring you. Where were you last night?"

"I… uh…"

"All I get is a text! 'Can't make it.' That's it! What was so important you had to cancel our date last night?"

Date? What the hell? She thought it was a date? I try to rewind to our conversation. But everything is muddy. Is this what sex does? Like a hangover without the feeling like crap part.

"Hello?"

I shake my head running a hand over the back of my neck. "Sorry, Quynn. I didn't realize… I thought… something came up, and I couldn't make it."

She rolls her eyes and stomps past me.

"Really, it's not just some excuse. A friend was having a bad night."

Girlfriend, Brody. Say it! Hayles is your girlfriend!

"A friend?" She cocks an eyebrow.

"Yeah."

Her arms drop, and she starts playing with her fingers. "Hayley?"

I nod. Guess Mom's not the only person who's noticed how much time I spend with her.

"It's not like that, though."

Whoa, what the hell? What am I saying? It's exactly like that. I just told Hayles loved her… after *making* love to her. I'm lying right into Quynn's face 'cause…

I don't know how to finish that thought.

"Not like what?"

Her eyes flick to mine, but I don't hold her stare. I go straight to looking at the crack in the porch.

"Nothing. Never mind."

"Okaaaay." She takes a step towards me, plastering on a smile. "Well, you're not skipping out on the one tonight. Promise?"

That word is just as bad as 'please'. And I'm still confused as hell why she still has such power over me when I'm in love with Hayles. But I'm nodding and she's hugging me, then she's gone.

Maybe douchebaggery is genetic.

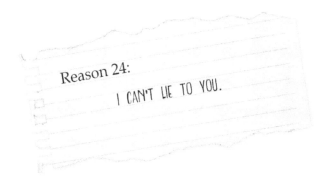

Reason 24:
I CAN'T LIE TO YOU.

"Hey, I know you hate the pop in, but—"

I stop Hayley from overanalyzing with a big kiss, 'cause really, ever since Quynn left it's all I've wanted to do.

"Whoa," she says, pushing back from me and turning red, "does this mean you're okay with me just coming over without calling?"

I smile and pull her inside. "I'll make an exception for you."

She folds her arms. "Oh no."

"What?"

"You're turning into a very cheesy sappy lovesick boy." She reaches up to feel my forehead. "What have I done?"

I knock her hand off, but keep her in my hold. "No cheesy stuff, huh? How about I just take you downstairs, and we'll do it."

She laughs. "There's the boy I knew was in there."

"Is that a yes?"

She shakes her head and plops on the couch. "I actually have a favor to ask."

I almost spout off an 'Anything for you', but the cheesy comment stops my mouth. Moving her legs off the end of the couch, I sit next to her, clasping my hand with hers.

"Okay, I know it's uber lame, but my friends, like, they all want to go on this big group date thing. I guess now that I have a boyfriend…" She flicks her eyes to meet mine, and I smile. Hell yeah, I'm her boyfriend. "They want me to come along. Well… *us* to come along."

"Sure. When?"

"That's the thing," she says, leaning her head against my shoulder, "I know we had plans tonight already, and I'm not sure what you had in store for me, but they wanted to meet up later. Can we fit that in?"

It's as if everything freezes right there, and I'm faced with the stupid choice again. Quynn or Hayles. I always choose Hayles, but then end up feeling guilty as crap over ditching Quynn. And I'd be doing it to her twice. I should've told her everything about me and Hayles. I should've said it as easily as Hayley just said it. I'm her boyfriend. She's my girlfriend.

Brody, you're a stupid ass.

"Hayley?"

"Uh oh." She sits up and looks me in the face. "Something's wrong. Spill."

I don't lie to Hayley. I can't. "Okay, don't be mad though."

There goes the cute eyebrow crinkle.

"Quynn came over earlier and asked if I'd go to Jamie's party tonight."

"Okay…"

"Well, I kind of ditched her last night, so I felt bad and I told her I'd go."

Her eyebrows go from crinkle to sky high. "You had a date with Quynn last night?"

"No!" I shift on the couch and grab her face, but she wiggles out from my hold. "Seriously, Hayles, it wasn't like that. I actually drove by your house to see if you would go with me."

She still doesn't relax. "Did you tell her?"

"What?"

"About us. That we're together."

I drop my eyes and shake my head, fingering the tatt on my wrist. "I… I tried."

Silence. Like too long silence. She stands up, pulling the sleeves down on her hoodie.

"What does it mean?"

Her voice is soft. Not mad, not sad, just passive. And it sucks.

"What does what mean?"

She points at my wrist. "Your tattoo."

I scratch the back of my neck, wanting to close the distance between me and Hayles, but I can't. Not after this crap.

"You got it for her, didn't you?"

Again, no anger, no sadness, just a 'who gives a crap?' attitude.

"It was a while ago, Hayles. It's not for her anymore."

"Then what does it mean?"

I finally unfreeze, close the distance between us and wrap her in my arms. She doesn't hug me back. "They are symbols of devotion," I whisper into her hair. "I don't want to be like my... my real dad. I made a promise I'd never hurt someone like he hurt my mom."

"Or like your brother hurt Quynn."

She says it into my chest and tries to pull away. I don't let her.

"Please, Hayles, I can't... I just didn't know how to..."

"You still like her." She forces herself out of my hold. "I knew you did. And please, don't be sorry or try to convince me that you don't. I don't regret anything we did. You've given me a lot, Brody. You're a good... friend. And that's all I expected from you."

"No." No. No. No. "You've got it wrong. I love *you*." I see it in her eyes. She's closing off. She's disappearing. She's leaving. And I can't stop her. What do I say to stop her? To make her realize? To get her to understand? "Don't leave. Don't run away from this."

Her eyes narrow, and finally some emotion erupts out of her. It's not a good one, but at least it's something.

"Stop lying to me! Stop trying to get me to believe you've chosen me over her. I'm not the girl guys go after. Especially guys like you. I knew that. I *knew* it! And I let myself fall for you anyway. I let you convince me you were better than all of them, but you're not. You're the same."

Heat shoots through my chest and I can't take it anymore. I'm yelling back at her as she goes for the door. "It's not me, Hayles. I've been honest. I do love you, but you won't let me. You're looking for ways out of this 'cause it's easier for you. Closing off 'cause you don't want to get hurt, but you know, you're missing out on something real. Me. You. Us. That's *real*. Stop blaming me, your mom, your weight, or whatever other delusion you have about me and Quynn. You are the one who's keeping us apart. Not me."

Her eyes are watering, and I want to eat all the words I've just said. She sniffles and says between hitched breaths, "I... gave... you... *all* of me. I let you in." She sniffs again, opens the door and steps out onto the porch. "And you can't even tell her you're with me. You can't tell anyone about me. I bet your best friend doesn't even know." She pauses to wipe more tears from her face. Tears I wish I hadn't put there. "You can't let her go."

It's quiet between us. I don't know what to say to make her feel better. Don't know what she's thinking. She's right. She knows it. But I'm right too.

Aren't I?

"I was telling the truth when I said I don't regret anything between us. You gave me the best few weeks of my life. I'm glad you were my first... everything."

She's saying goodbye. No. No. No.

"Hayley, don't—"

"You deserve someone who you can brag about to your friends. Someone who's not embarrassing to be with. Someone who you want to shout out to the world you love them." She gulps. "It's just not me."

Before I can argue, before I can do anything, she turns and leaves, huddling into the hoodie I gave her last night.

I should chase after her. That's what they want, right? Girls always want the guy to chase them down and beg and plead to take them back.

Instead I fall on the porch steps, bury my face, and let go of the first tears I've ever cried over a girl.

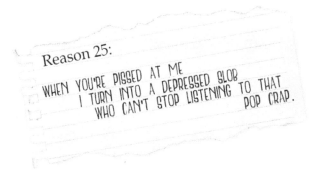

Reason 25:
WHEN YOU'RE PISSED AT ME
I TURN INTO A DEPRESSED SLOB
WHO CAN'T STOP LISTENING TO THAT
POP CRAP.

It's the ass room again. I did go to that party, came home and crashed on the bed and stayed there till Mom and Dad came home. It's amazing how in the course of twenty-four hours, my room is stock full of dirty laundry and pizza boxes.

And I don't give a shit.

The whole time at the party I wanted to tell Quynn. I wanted to be straight with her. *I'm with Hayley. Sorry if I gave you the wrong idea.* But the words never came out. 'Cause I'm not with Hayles. Not anymore. Or was I ever?

So I drank myself into a stupor, and I've spent all day burping up pizza and garlic bread, and listening to Katy Perry on repeat.

"I'm never leaving you alone again." Mom comes in and whips open the window. I groan and throw the pillow over my head. "Have you even left this room today?"

"Just to piss," I mumble into the mattress. They took a cab home since I didn't get my ass out of bed to pick 'em up like I'd planned. I was going to have Hayley come with me, but that was before things went to the crapper.

The pillow gets ripped off my head.

"Uh oh." Mom goes to sit on my bed, but changes her mind when she spots a pizza slice stuck to the sheets. "Um..." She swallows back whatever chunks rose in her throat. "What happened, honey?"

Not going to talk about this with my mom. So I give her a "Nothing" and turn my face back into the mattress.

"Don't you dare lie to me. I'd throw a tomato in your face, but right now I doubt it would do anything."

She's right. I may puke, but I puked all morning, so I couldn't give a damn right now.

"Did something happen with Gabe?"

I shake my head, but it gives me a headache so I stop.

"Quynn?"

"Ma, I don't want to talk about it."

"So it *is* about Quynn."

I grab the back of my head and try to force my face farther into the bed. It's not doing anything though. Just making my temples ache. Doesn't hurt as much as what's going on in my chest though.

"She'll come around. She's always liked you."

"It's not that, Mom. Please, just leave it alone."

"You know I won't do that."

Why is it so hard? Why is it hard to talk about Hayley in a 'more than friends' way?

I know why. I just don't want to admit it even to myself. Because it would make me a dumbass. A hypocritical dumbass.

I don't want to see the look on people's faces when I tell them I'm in love with the… FFF.

But this is Mom. She'll keep pushing and pushing till I've leaked out all my insides.

"It's not Quynn." I turn around so I'm talking to the ceiling. "It's Hayley."

"Oh!"

Her shock whenever I say Hayley's name is getting old. And I won't look at her. I don't want to see her expression.

"Come on, Mom. You had to have figured out I liked her."

"Actually, honey, I didn't. You never talked about her really. Just referred to her as a friend, a signing partner. I haven't even officially met her yet. Only saw her from a distance, and she didn't seem like your type of girl."

My forehead crinkles, and I look at her. "What do you mean by that?" I'm snapping. This is why I didn't want to say anything.

She shrugs and waves her hand through the air. "Ah, nothing. Just first impression."

After watching her for a few seconds, trying to figure out if she's lying to me, I give up and put my head back down on the pillows.

"She's amazing. Been through a bunch of crap, but still manages to be just so… awesome. She's fun, funny, it's never awkward around her. All the crap with Gabe, with my grades, all the other stuff going on that sucks, just goes away when I'm around her. I'm a better person when I'm with her. Less angry."

It's quiet, except for Mom's breathing and me trying to push back the tears I thought I had cried out already.

"I messed up. I was too afraid to tell Quynn about her. Too scared to tell anyone about her. I don't know why."

I sit up, leaning my elbows on my knees. "I love her, Mom. How do I fix it?"

She gives me a big grin. One of those, 'silly boy, the answer is staring you in the face' smiles. A Mom smile.

"That's easy, hun."

"It is?"

She nods. "You've already done what she needs from you."

"I have?"

"You told *me* about her." She comes to the side of my bed and rubs my arm. I don't shrug her off. "All she wants is to know you're in this one-hundred percent before she lets go completely. Girls are very protective of their hearts. They need to know their guy won't be ashamed to show them off, kiss them in public, and of course, she needs to know you're over any… old flames."

She pinches my elbow. I pull it back and give her a glare.

"If you can't tell Quynn about Hayley, then maybe you don't love her as much as you think you do."

Ouch, Mom. But, crap, she's right.

I nod and scrape off the pizza stuck to my sheets and throw it in an empty box on the floor. Mom makes a face before grabbing the garbage and getting to the doorway.

"Oh, and honey?"

"Yeah?"

"I didn't peg you for a Katy Perry fan." She ducks out the door as my pillow goes flying across the room at her.

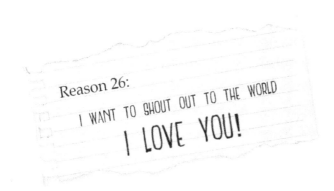

Reason 26:
I WANT TO SHOUT OUT TO THE WORLD
I LOVE YOU!

"Game night again, dude?" Tanner shoves the rest of his pizza in his mouth and wipes his hands on his jeans before letting me inside. It's been a whole week since I slept with Hayles, and then tore her heart up the next day. School's been weird. Quynn's been distant, but giving me the 'are you okay?' look every time she glances in my direction. And Hayles has gone back to being my 'homie'. Like nothing happened. It's worse than her ignoring me. It's like I didn't put a dent in her at all. But she's a good actress. So she's probably hurting more than she's saying.

I probably should've called before coming over to Tanner's but not so good at the phone thing. Pretty sure Hayles is the only exception I make to call someone.

"Nah," I say, marching straight to the fridge. "I got something to do tonight. Just killing time before."

Truth is, I'm nervous as hell and I need a distraction. And Tanner has more junk food than Mom keeps stocked in our house.

"Quynn? You finally going for it, man?"

I take a swig of Pepsi, clear my throat and avoid his eyes. "Uh, no. Hayley. I'm going to swing by, see if she's home."

I hold my breath, waiting for his reaction, but I really should give Tanner more credit, 'cause he punches my shoulder and says,

"Hell yeah, man. You guys should hang out here again." He winks and goes to plop on his couch. I grab a slice of pizza from the box on the counter and join him.

"So..." Dude, talking chicks, even with the best friend gets a little awkward, but I'm nervous and I've already talked the crap out of it with my family. "What do you think about her?"

"She's cool. Any girl who can kick my ass at Ghost Recon is okay in my book." He turns on the TV and tosses his legs up on the coffee table. "You guys a thing now?"

I wish. "Nah, but... maybe soon."

"You like her?"

He's not looking at me, or showing much interest, but it makes answering easier. "Yeah."

"Cool." He flips through the channels, one hand tucked behind his head. "Then a rematch is definitely in the cards. Don't screw up tonight, Bro."

***

Quynn.

Her name used to send a different kind of wave through my body, but right now, it makes me sick. No matter what I do, I'm hurting someone. But that's my fault, not theirs. If only I had manned up and told Quynn right away. Told her I was falling hard and fast for Hayles. Stopped dragging her around, making her feel like I still felt the same way.

And I'm not like Gabe. I'm not like my dad. Which is why I'm telling her now. Not 'cause I'm trying to make things better with Hayles, but because it's the right thing to do.

I gotta let her go... all the way.

"Hey, Bro."

She sits down on the grass next to me, staring out at the sprinklers going off in the soccer field at the park.

"Hey, Quynn."

Her arm loops through mine, and she leans her head on my shoulder. "Are you finally going to tell me what's been bothering you all week?"

180

I turn my head toward her. She's beautiful, always has been, and I don't know if I'm ready to see the hurt in her face. The same hurt when she caught my brother cheating on her. But then I remind myself... I'm stopping this before it gets to that. We weren't ever together. Haven't been on a date. Haven't kissed. Never told each other how we feel. As much as I liked her in the past, when I look at her now, all I see is my friend.

And that's when it gets easy. The words are easy now. I don't know why they weren't before. Why I held them back from her. Why I held them from anyone. I *do* wanna do that cheesy junk. Shout it out from the rooftops and crap like that.

"I'm in love with Hayley."

Her eyes get real big as she takes her head off my shoulder. "Really?"

I nod. "I-I've got it bad."

Her lips part, and she mouths, 'Wow', but I don't hear anything.

"I'm sorry if... I don't know if you thought we... I mean, I used to... I really wanted to..."

Bumbling idiot. These words aren't easy.

She saves me by putting a hand to my lips. "It's okay, Brody. I knew something was up. I thought you were mad at me, but you were just trying to protect me, weren't you?"

I take her hand and pull it from my mouth. "Yeah. I didn't want you thinking I was the same as G—"

"You are *not* your brother." She pats my leg, just like she used to do when we were closer friends. "You are much better than him." Her lips pull up in a smile, and she rubs my buzzed head noogie-style. "Why didn't you tell me sooner? I wouldn't have pushed you into hanging out with me so much. Probably didn't make things easier."

I didn't say anything 'cause apparently, I don't give people enough credit. No one is reacting the way I thought they would. I expected to get a crap lecture about how Quynn is better for me from Mom, a wiseass comment and some razzing from Tanner, and heartache and a punch in the face from Quynn. Now that I think

REASONS I FELL FOR THE FUNNY FAT FRIEND

about it, I screwed up the one thing I wanted most 'cause I didn't think people would see what I see in Hayles. They'd be like her judgmental mom.

I should've known better. After all, I'm the one who kept telling her to shut up 'cause she's beautiful, and fun, funny, and... awesomesauce.

A smile breaks through, and I'm suddenly laughing at myself. Laughing so hard I think I'm scaring Quynn.

"What is so funny?"

I shake my head as more chuckles come out. "I'm an idiot."

She laughs with me now. "Well, that's what love does to you."

In the words of Hayles... cheeseball. But a cheeseball who's right.

I tuck her into a big hug, smothering her face in my chest like I used to and wiggle her hair back and forth. "Thanks for being so cool."

"Thanks for being honest, Bro." She ducks out from underneath me. "Now will you please go get your girl before I beat you to it."

I give her a pervy cock of the head. "Really? I'd like to see that."

She punches me in the arm. "I mean it. Go!" Then she pushes me. I stumble to my feet.

"Thanks, Quynn. And I'm sorry if I gave you the wrong idea. Really... I didn't ever want to hurt you. And I'm sorry if I did."

Half her mouth pulls up. "You couldn't hurt me even if you tried." She waves me off. "Please don't let me get in the way of what I can tell, is head over heels lovey dovey stuff."

I chuckle, study her face once more before taking off down the road, finally feeling guilt free about leaving Quynn behind me.

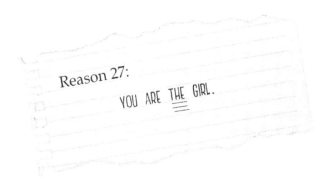

Reason 27:
YOU ARE THE GIRL.

I knock on the door quick, then shove my hands in my jeans. She makes me nervous. Real nervous. The good kind of nervous. The kind that makes me want to jump and not care about what happens.

That was real sappy. I've become a love-crazed sonnet spewing sucker. Just like everyone else who figures out what they want.

The handle turns and I'm about to do a one-knee-er 'cause I'm that big of a sap now, but it's judgmental mom.

"May I help you?"

She acts as if she doesn't know who I am. I know she does. She's given me those pissy stares since I first locked eyes with her.

"Is Hayley home?"

Her hand moves to the back of the door. The ready position to slam it in my face. I tuck my foot in the doorway. "She's busy. You can see her at school."

"Please, I need to talk to her. It's important."

She lets out a dismissive laugh that sounds like a grunt in her Cruella voice. "What is so important you have to distract her from her exercises?"

I lied. Quynn wasn't the hardest one to tell. It's Hayles' mother. I scratch the back of my neck and gulp.

"I love her."

If she had been drinking anything, it would've been sprayed all over my face. I get a little spit anyway when her mouth pops open, and she 'gah's' at me.

"Excuse me? Who do you think you are?"

"My name's Brody Grant."

"I know *who* you are. But are you blind? Maybe a little slow in the head? Or just looking for someone to roll around with till you leave for college?"

Whoa, whoa, whoa. What kind of parent talks like this?

"Why would you ask that?" I say through my teeth.

"You're taking advantage of my daughter. I don't know what you're using her for, but I won't allow it. No one with your…" She gestures to my body and lets the thought drop. I cross my arms. "Would spend time with my Hayley without an agenda."

Heat is crawling through my chest, begging to be unleashed. I choke back the insult I've got for her, and try to come up with something that doesn't have the word 'bitch' in it.

"You must not know me that well, then." *Bitch.* "I'm in love with your daughter because she's the best thing that's happened to me. She's smart, funny, and has a *kickass* body. And I'm not going to hide her till I find her 'acceptable'. She's already perfect. And I don't care what you think. I'm telling her that."

I shove past her, ignoring the protests and the threats to call the cops if I'm not outta there in five minutes. I go straight to Hayles' room. She's lying on the floor, headphones in her ears, eyes closed and tears going down the sides of her face and landing in her hair. She's singing. Soft and beautiful, and I'm amazed I know the song. It's from a musical. Judge me all you want, but I know Les Miserables.

I close the door behind me. Judgmental mom gave me five minutes. I'm going to make them count. Lying on the floor, heads together and feet facing opposite directions, I wipe a tear from her eye as she sings the last note.

She jumps, sitting straight up and holding her chest.

"Holy frigging fruitbats. You scared the snot out of me."

"Sorry." I smile. I'm not sorry at all.

She punches me in the shoulder, doing that friend act she's been keeping up all week. "Whatcha doing here, Mr. Grant?" Her eyes go to her door like she's finally realizing I'm in her room. "Oh my gosh, *how* did you get up here?"

"I dodged past your mom."

She laughs. A Hayley laugh. "You are crazy. What is so important you couldn't just text me?"

I jump to my feet and reach for her hands, which suddenly need to be in her pockets. I smirk at her, take her wrists and pull them from her pants, trapping them in mine.

She's not getting away this time.

"I told her."

"What?"

"I told Quynn that I'm in love with you."

Her face gets real red. That damn cute red that drives me crazy. "Um, why would you do that?"

I shake my head, smiling at her. "'Cause it's the truth, you dork."

"And... you're okay with that? You're... happy?"

She sounds like it's a hard concept to grasp. That I'm happy to be in love with the most amazing girl I've ever met.

I let go of one of her hands to jam mine in my back pocket. I pull out the worn piece of paper. The one that's been read and re-read so many times so I've got them all memorized. The one I keep adding things to because there are just so many reasons why I want her. Why she's *the* girl.

"Hayles," I say, tucking the paper into her palm, "this is the first list of many I plan on writing for you. Whatever it takes to let you know how incredible you are, I'll do it. You don't have to be with me if that's not what you want, but you should know how much you mean to someone. How important you are."

Her mouth splits open into her Hayley smile. The one that goes right up to her dark green eyes. "My list?" She tugs me to the bed, plops us down, her hands shaking as she opens it.

185

"You're going to read it now?"

"Duh!" She giggles. "I've been waiting for it. I didn't think I'd get it after… you know." She waves it off like our argument was nothing more than just a tiny spat. I laugh, putting my arm behind her and reading over her shoulder even though I know them all.

She's laughing, and the smile on her face doesn't leave. She gasps at number twenty-three and slaps me in the arm. But by the end of the list, she's practically in my lap, hand on my leg and tears in her eyes, but not like the ones she had a few minutes ago.

"Brody?"

"Yeah?"

She takes a deep breath and turns to face me, her leg separating us from being as close as I want to be.

"I'm sorry."

I raise an eyebrow. "What do you have to be sorry for?"

Another deep breath. "You were right. It was me who was keeping us apart. I… I didn't want to love you because I was afraid you'd wake up and realize what a cow you've chosen for a girlfriend."

"Hayles—"

"Sorry, I won't do that anymore. After reading this, I get it."

Something in my chest tightens. And I want to pull her into me, but I wait for her to finish.

"I guess I *am* pretty awesome."

I laugh, and that's it for my self control. Cupping her face in my hands, I pull her mouth to mine, letting her smile and kiss me at the same time. I like that. She's happy to be kissing me.

And I'm smiling too. Even when judgmental mom comes in, I wave her off, giving her a 'one more minute' finger. But yeah, that woman is a lot stronger than I thought she would be. She pulls me from the room and tosses me down the stairs and out the front door.

I'm about to drive away when Hayles comes running down the driveway, ignoring the Cruella Devil screams behind her and plops in the seat next to me.

"I want another one." She smiles, and I give her what she wants. She can have *everything* she wants.

She pulls back, then buckles her seatbelt and tosses her feet on the dash. Her hand goes right for the stereo. "Where to, Mr. Grant?"

"How long do you have?"

"As long as you want."

I put the car in gear and pull out onto the road. "Feel like meeting my parents?"

"They're home?"

I smirk. "They will be, in about three hours."

She tucks her hand in mine, giving me an evil grin. "I think we can pump one out in three hours."

I speed the rest of the way home.

Epilogue

"You look da… dang sexy. Stop freaking out."

Hayles fixes her hair one more time in the sideview mirror before standing up. "You sure? I've never done something like this."

I step back to study her outfit. She hates it when I do this. When I let my eyes rake over every curve, every part of her, and yeah, I check out her boobs way longer than she likes, but can you blame me?

"Knock it off, you perv!" She punches my arm and I grab her hand, pulling her toward me.

"Don't ask me to check you out if you don't mean it."

She rolls her eyes. "You'll do it anyway."

"Is that a bad thing?"

Another punch. I laugh and kiss her, stopping her from answering me with another wiseass comment. She's good at it. The kissing and the comments.

"Okay, I think I'm ready."

"You sure you don't want to just, stay in?"

She shakes her head. "You're supposed to be showing me off!"

"I know, I know."

I wrap my hand around her waist, and pull her to the restaurant. Mom and Dad are in there, probably talking about why I asked them to meet me and Hayles here. Mom going into all these cheesy romantic things while Dad's pretending to listen, but really wanting a drink.

"Hayley!"

Mom has adopted Hayles. It's good for them, I know. Mom wanting that daughter, and Hayley needing a mom who doesn't care what size pants she wears. Still, I wish she wouldn't hog my girlfriend so much.

They hug, and I pull Hayley's chair out for her. She still blushes whenever I do stuff guys are supposed to do. Wonder if she'll ever get used to it.

"Okay, okay, tell us! Are you two getting married?" Mom's enthusiasm and assumption makes me spit the water I just put in my mouth all over Dad.

"Thanks a lot." He grabs a napkin and wipes his face off, chuckling behind it.

"No, Mom. We're not getting married. We just graduated."

"Some people do that you know." She smiles and winks at Hayles, whose blush has not disappeared.

"Not us. We do the whole marriage thing without the rings first."

Oh no. She's not telling my parents about our sex life.

"You know, fight and threaten to throw clothes out on the lawn." She smiles. "And if he doesn't put the seat down next time, I'm nailing it to the toilet."

They all laugh, including me.

"All right, so no marriage. But tell me what it is! I'm dying!" Mom bounces up and down in her seat, and so does Hayles, matching her excitement. Dad laughs behind his glass.

"Well, I got into U of O," I stutter.

Mom grabs Hayley—not me—into a big hug and Dad claps a hand on my back.

"That's great, kid."

"Thanks."

Mom lets go of Hayles, whose face has permanently turned the color of those tomatoes Mom threatens me with, and says, "Congratulations! And that's close too so we can still visit you and Hayley."

Whoa, wait a second. Do they think…?

"We're not going to live together." Hayles giggles, saving me from that conversation. "Just going to be in the same school. You know, so I can help him pass his classes." She nudges me, and I keep her hand. Don't know why she gets so nervous about every date. I guess I'd be nervous if I went out with her and her parents, but she's so good at everything.

The rest of dinner goes pretty much how it goes at home. Mom and Dad embarrassing me while Hayles joins in occasionally, but her hand stays on my knee, letting me know she does it all 'cause she loves me.

I tell Mom and Dad I'll be out late, and they give me those stupid looks like, 'we know, we know' and then hugs, then they take off. I help Hayles into the Dodge—my Dodge—and her feet are on the dash before I even get in.

The drive isn't silent, since she sings the whole time. I don't mind that there's no conversation. This is our thing.

I pull up to the apartments just around the corner from U of O. Hayles got a roommate as soon as she found out she was going there and moved out about two seconds after that.

She still hasn't met Daniel, but she doesn't seem to care.

"Will you come inside?" She unbuckles. "I have something for you."

I'm always up for the invitation to go in with her, but from her expression I know I'm not getting lucky tonight.

"Sure."

The apartment is small, but big enough for her and her roommate. Hayles doesn't have a lot of stuff. And she's just starting work to pay for it all. She does have a bed though. That's important.

"Where's Callie?" Roommate.

She shrugs. "Not here, I guess."

Hmm… maybe I will get lucky. She's dragging me to her room.

I go for her mouth when she closes the door, but she puts a hand over it, making me make out with the back of her hand.

"Not yet, impatient boy."

She said yet...

She slips under my arm and goes for her nightstand. She takes out a piece of paper that looks like the list I gave her months ago. Smiling her Hayley smile, she puts it in my hand.

"These are my reasons."

"You made a list?"

She nods, smile still glued on her face.

"Gosh darn it, Brody. I love the heck out of you. You should know why too."

I don't read it. Not yet. I tuck it in my back pocket and kiss her. She growls and pushes me off.

"You don't like it?" She fake pouts.

I shake my head. "You want me to read it right now?" I kiss her neck, watching her skin pop up with goose bumps.

She moans. "You're such a cheater."

I trace her jaw line with my lips, wrapping my arms around her middle and laying her flat on the bed.

"Right now, right now? Or can it wait for—"

"Two minutes?" She giggles, and I grunt at her. "Kidding! Kidding!" She laughs again.

Her hand dips into my back pocket while mine goes up her shirt. I know what will distract her.

The paper gets shoved over my eyes, and my arm gets pulled out from her shirt. I'm not going to win this one.

"All right, all right, stubborn girl. I'll read it now." I sit up, adjusting myself so I'm comfortable. She snuggles into the crook of my neck, reading over my shoulder.

There's one thing on the list. And it's in big letters, and I bark out my laughter.

YOU'RE GOOD IN THE SACK.

"You dork." I toss the paper over my shoulder, and she laughs against my lips.

"Thought that would be the only one you cared about."

I shake my head, wiggling my nose against hers. It still amazes me that she's *my* girl.

"Hayles?"

"Sup?"

I chuckle, tucking her hair back. How did I get here? How did I end up being the guy she lets in? I don't know what I did, but I'm glad I get to do it. Every time I catch her looking at her reflection. She's pulling skin, pinching and prodding areas on her body with such a defeated look on her face, and she lets me whip her around, tell her how beautiful she is and kiss her until she's smiling again. I get to do that for her, and in exchange I got the sexiest girl, the funniest girl, the smartest girl...

Damn, I'm lucky.

I give her one more kiss before I ask, "Did you have enough dairy today?"

The End

ACKNOWLEDGMENTS

Thank you spell check, for helping me spell not only half the words in this book, but also 'Acknowledgments'.

Thank you reader, for picking up my book and staying with it all the way to this page.

Thank you Mommy, for yelling at me on a daily basis to get this book in the world.

Thank you late night fast food, for knowing sometimes a ninety-nine cent taco at midnight will help cure writer's block.

Thank you critique partners (Gosh, so many… Abby, Hope, Jade, Jenny, Kelley, Theresa) for telling me when Brody sounded like a girl, and when he acted like one. And most importantly, thank you for falling in love with Hayley.

Thank you Suzi, for telling me where all my commas should go. I'm sure there are a million misplaced ones on this page alone.

Thank you Jolene, for my original awesomesauce cover, and for calling me at eleven o'clock one night, giving me the extra push I needed to be braver than I am.

Thank you to Allie for my updated awesomesauce cover, which I can't wait to share with the world!

Thank you to my sisters, for reading this book a million times, calling me to quote it, and basically making my head a thousand times bigger than it was before.

Thank you children, for not caring about Mommy 'writing out loud' when I give you baths or cook your food.

And lastly, thank you to my hubber bubber, for falling for the funny fat friend.

ALSO BY CASSIE MAE

Young Adult
Reasons I Fell for the Funny Fat Friend
You Can't Catch Me
Friday Night Alibi
Secret Catch

YA Series
How to Date a Nerd
How to Seduce a Band Geek
How to Hook a Bookworm

King Sized Beds and Happy Trails
Beach Side Beds and Sandy Paths
Lonesome Beds and Bumpy Roads
True Love and Magic Tricks

New Adult
Switched
The Real Thing
Unexpectedly You
Broken Records

Romance
Doing It for Love
No Interest in Love
Crazy About Love
Flirty Thirty
Make Lemonade

Coming Soon!
Pillowtalk (April 2017)
Stage Kissed (May 2017)

ABOUT CASSIE MAE

Cassie Mae is the author of a dozen or so books. Some of which became popular for their quirky titles, characters, and stories. She likes writing about nerds, geeks, the awkward, the fluffy, the short, the shy, the loud, the fun.

Since publishing her bestselling debut, Reasons I Fell for the Funny Fat Friend, she's published several titles with Penguin Random House and founded **CookieLynn Publishing Services**. She is represented by Sharon Pelletier at Dystel and Goderich Literary Management. She has a favorite of all her book babies, but no, she won't tell you what it is. (Mainly because it changes depending on the day.)

Along with writing, Cassie likes to binge watch Once Upon A Time and The Flash. She can quote Harry Potter lines quick as a whip. And she likes kissing her hubby, but only if his facial hair is trimmed. She also likes cheesecake to a very obsessive degree.

You can stalk, talk, or send pictures of Luke Bryan to her on her Facebook page: https://www.facebook.com/cassiemaeauthor

Made in the USA
Las Vegas, NV
19 February 2021